LEVITATING: STORIES

GAGE GREENWOOD

For Heather Hinton Field, who selflessly gives, who creates the gateways into reading, who builds the bridges for those who need access to books, and who works tirelessly to bring fun and love and knowledge to her community.

THE SUPERSTARS OF PATREON

The following people make this writing career of mine possible. If you enjoyed this book, thank them. Without their support, it wouldn't be possible. They truly are my heroes.

SIGNAL SENDERS: Michael Casey, Rebecca Rogers

WHITE WOLVES: Jamie Rose, Sarah Pruitt, Jamie McFarland, Meghan Burns, Molly Mix, Kirsty Williams , Emily Morash

WINTER'S LEGENDS: Mari Pittelman, Chana Odom, Cayley Gimelli, Nicole Laudij, Savannah Fischer , Mary Trujillo, Jennifer Sweet, Teresa, Damaris Quinones, Carrie Hibbard, Chaz Williams, Amy Porter, Charlotte Stevenson, Kelly Jobes , Tracy Allen, Engilbert Egill Steffonsson, Kylee Jones, Lisa Vasquez, Chris Knickerbocker, Angie Valentine, Kristina Lee, Rhonda Bobbitt , Ali Sweet, Kendall OConnor, Sara Ferrarese. Megan Stockton, Sophia McIntyre, Adam Fischer, Gale Grindstaff, Heather Hinton Field,

DEMIGODS: Alicia Toothman, Lauren, Jacinta Williams, Tiqua Lovett, A.K. Daver, Jason Artz, Janalyn prude, Milt Theodossiou, Kristal Shanahan,

LAMPPOSTS: Allia Kennedy, John Durgin, Emmie Stone, April Butler, Erin Grosch, Margo Dearborn, Ashley

Protus, Jay Bower, Candace Nola, John Lynch, Lindalaine, NRD, Kate Stevenson, Trina Thompson, Alexandria Bracanovich, Elyn Noble, Stephanie Huddle, Dagan Boyd, Nicole Laudij, Roth Schilling, Kelli Hahn, Sally Feliz, Chiara Cooper, Justine Manzano, jl courtney, Sarah D'Ambro, Shannon Jack, Alexandrea Christenson, Amber Reed

HUSKS: Asia BeeGee, Andrea Johnson, Brianna Van Riet, Stacie Denise, Kristina Lebedeva, Erica Kennedy, Tiffany Riggs, Summer Smith, Brooke Conley, Amber Conley, Jaxon Lee Rose, S.P. Somtow (Somtow Sucharitkul), Shannon Ettaro

Join the Party: www.patreon.com/gagegreenwood

WARNING

The stories in this collection are so shocking, we require you to sign this waiver before flipping this page: I, _______________, hereby agree not to hold the author accountable for any hair loss, sore throats from screaming, weird new sexual fetishes, or any other adverse effects the book may cause.

Also, this is a Gage Greenwood book, so most of that stuff is utter bullshit. It contains a normal level of horror. Nothing too shocking. Maybe a bit depressing at points. Why the hell is Gage always so depressing in his writing, but so damned goofy on his social media accounts? It's almost like he's trying to be one of those sad clowns. You know what I mean? Anyway, to hell with him. Enjoy the collection.

Here's what you *will* find: violence, self-harm, some sex stuff, murder most foul, drug and alcohol abuse, really rude commentary on some pop culture stuff that you won't agree with, appreciative commentary on some pop culture stuff that you probably hate and it'll make you angry that I like it because you just can't understand how anyone could enjoy that crap, the occasional ambiguous ending that will piss you off, and typical Gageisms, like how many times will he mention Kevin Friggin' Bacon? It wasn't even funny the first time.

TWO SHOWS ON SATURDAY

My apartment is two things, what it is and what it once was, and those two things conflate in my mind like overlapping alternate dimensions.

Ringlets from my mother's coffee cup stain the glass table in front of the couch, and the brown rug under it is thick with Luna's fur. Those things are real, tangible, ghosts with substance.

The other ghosts are just for me.

My mother will show up, lounging on the couch in her bathrobe, doing the crossword with the Game Show Network playing in the background, or hovering over her computer, absorbed in her pay-to-play computer games. She never looks at me. Not anymore.

Then there's the dog. Luna's pitter-pattering feet echo behind me wherever I walk. When it's quiet, I swear I can hear his teeth grinding on the entertainment center's peeling wood veneer. His sounds are as solid as any piece of furniture.

To the left of my bedroom, an arched doorway opens into my mother's room. No matter how much disinfectant I've used, I can never scrub from my brain the olfactory nightmare that room once was. When I pass the threshold, wafts of piss and shit, sweat and sickness storm my nose.

I keep my head down. Too many ghosts, too many thoughts. I'm afraid of the drab colors, and the memories of my mother's Boston Terrier, his head listing toward me with droopy eyes, begging me to step up, to wake up and to take him outside.

In the kitchen, I toss my keys on the table next to a microphone and recording equipment, stuff I purchased for a podcast I never started. More ghosts: half-fulfilled ambitions. They keep growing and I can't bear the weight.

I don't bother putting the six-pack in the fridge. I'll kill the beers before they warm up. The first sip removes the pressure from my brain. The scream I'd been wanting to release dies in my throat.

On a notepad, I scribble down my set:

> *I'm an alcoholic.*
> *Alcoholic steps.*
> *My mom wants grandkids.*
> *Diet.*
> *Blah, blah, blah.*
> *Hospice.*
> *Etc. etc. etc.*

When I'm done, I fold the notepad and put it in my pocket. I'll only need it if I get too wasted. I pace the kitchen with a beer in hand, reciting my jokes from memory, planning the segues, darting from punchline to tag, and I'm good, quick, articulate, ready to crush.

I know it won't stay this way. The sharp edge, the reflexive pacing, the timing, it will all erode with the alcohol. It doesn't stop me from drinking, but at least I'm cognizant of my failings.

Tonight needs to be special. It needs to be perfect, but I'm not ready. I'll give it my best, and that's not much. I've had nothing left in my system since I lost Luna. My mother's death was a punch to the gut, but losing the dog was a chainsaw to my soul. It ruined me, and it continues to fuck me up every undeserved second I have on this earth.

I come to the club a few hours before show time. The bartender is there, a short, plucky girl covered in tattoos. She tells me the owner is around, but I don't see him anywhere. He's probably locked away in his office.

She pours me a tall vodka and coke, a freebie, but just this one. Without a crowd, the club feels like a coffin. Black paneled walls. Black paneled bar. Dim lights. Hollow. I need to puke.

I pass by fliers for upcoming shows as I head to the bathroom. Maria Bamford, Kyle Kinane, Doug Stanhope, comedians who matter, whose styles will be emulated, and will change the way comedy is looked at, the way it is understood.

I splash my face while sucking in big gulps of air. I don't think I can do this.

As I pass the manager's office, he calls me in. I get a small pat on the shoulder as I sit in the chair he pulls out for me. The silence, while brief, is crushing. He scans me. The red streaks in my eyes, the sickly pallor, the unshaven face. I know what he sees.

He gives me a pep talk, which is a dog-whistled threat hidden under the guise of inspiration. I hide my shaking hands under his desk. It's not the fear making them shake, it's my neurons misfiring, desperate for a drink.

After his speech, he stands, pats me again. "You got this."

I don't have this. I'm losing control, and his pep talk jerked the yoke into a nosedive.

His ultimate words of motivation. "Last chance."

The seats fill fast.

I stand on the side of the stage, leaning against a wall, two circular black tables in front of me, their seats packed with folks drinking beers from plastic bottles that look like caricaturized bullets.

They're laughing, most of them, the host performing his duties well. The untrained ear would only pick up the roars of approval, but I can't help noticing the shifting, settling, the clinking glasses, the rough sounds of metallic chair legs against the tiled floor.

I'm terrified. *Last chance.*

The manager. My mother. Luna. *Last chance.* I've had too many.

The host turns to me and exaggerates my qualifications, stretching his arm forward as if I am a shiny new car and he's the salesman. My nervous pout tidal waves into an artificial smile, and I scoot my way around the tables, hoping the applause drowns out the sound of my slamming heart.

The host shakes my hand and whispers, "Good luck" in my ear. We've worked together many times; he knows my act, knows my abilities, and like the club owner who's watching from the sound booth with his arms tucked into his pits, knows I'm a gamble.

I've never actually fucked up in this club, but the scene is small, and reputations carry. Everyone knows about the nights I was too drunk to care, stumbling on punchlines, stepping on laughs, and a few times, literally falling off the stage. There were two occasions where I needed to be carried off, dragged to the greenroom, clinging to a mic that had been shut off during one of my infamous drunken tirades about my fucking dog.

Luna. If I talk about Luna, it's over.

I'm the feature tonight. No goddamn way they'd let me headline. This weekend's headliner is a local guy with a middling career, and that's why I'm given any opportunity at all. The manager was already taking a chance; might as well make the entire show a gamble.

If I do well tonight, I'll be back for two shows tomorrow, but no one is counting on that, not even me.

I grab the mic, and I am swallowed whole by an orb of light. The spotlight sunders the room, allowing me to see only what's directly to my sides, deluging the long swaths of tables in front with ethereal white. I feel the light's warmth and squint at its magnitude.

I open with a self-deprecating joke, a bizarre one I hadn't planned in my set.

"Man, I've been depressed lately. Just sad. All the time. It's gotten so bad I've become a cutter."

Silence. Brows scrunch. People look to their neighbors, confused.

"Yeah, but the thing is, I don't like pain, so I cut other people instead."

Laughs. It's that easy tonight.

"Come here, asshole. I'm sad."

I make a slashing motion as if I am slicing someone's throat, and the crowd dies in a fit of laughter.

I relax. Not sure if it's the alcohol or the fact I got a few laughs, but my muscles ease, the tense grip I have on the mic loosens, and my chest expands. Maybe I can do this.

And then the ghosts appear.

My eyes adjust to the heavy spotlight. The room coalesces. I can't believe what I'm seeing. I can't believe it. This isn't real. It isn't fucking real.

Within the beam of light, there are smoky heads with

tangled bodies streaming around one another in a quasi-sexual spider web. Horrendous figures, translucent, spiraling, spinning around and within each other. It's dizzying. A wave of panic fires up the base of my spine and spews from my mouth with a horrific moan.

What the fuck is happening to me? Stroke? Alcohol-induced hallucinations? Mania? Madness? A rush of blood and fear builds in my skull, pressing into my temples. I might pass out.

Somehow, as I am hypnotized by these heads shimmying around one another, causing their clouded torsos to weave into a smoky tapestry, I pick up an uncomfortable cough from the crowd. They're waiting. How could I notice such an inane thing?

My hands tremble. Tears form in my eyes. The ghosts screech, and I wince, horrified by the high-pitched chorus. My mind automatically thinks about how it's going to fuck up my timing. Why do I care about my timing? How is that on my mind?

My eyes are laser-focused on the bright light and the scrim creatures swimming in it, but I can *feel* the crowd, their discomfort, their need for me to continue. Chairs scuff the floor, the audience shifting with nerves. They're all I have left. I can't ruin my relationship with them. This is it. This room, this mic, this me, this is all I have. All I am.

I pull myself from the light and mask my terror by smiling at a table of women. Two of them are wearing phallic balloons on their heads. Maybe they don't see my tears, or the trembling.

"Bachelorette party?" My voice is hoarse.

They shriek affirmative, and for a moment it drowns out the ghosts, but the ghosts seem to know this, and they react with louder screeches.

Tears are streaming down my face, but no one can see.

It's a goddamned bachelorette party, and I asked the question as if I had some gem of a joke for them, but I didn't. I have nothing.

I need something. I need it quickly. They're waiting.

In the corner of my eye, the movement in the light turns jerky and more rabid. Something is happening, but I can't look. I can't. Not right now.

The audience needs me. I need them.

"It's a bachelorette party, and you came to a damned comedy show?"

They giggle at themselves. The ghosts scream.

"Sorry ladies. I'm sure you wanted male strippers, and my name is Mike, but there is nothing magic about this."

I lift my shirt to reveal my flabby belly. Home run. The crown cracks up. Jesus, I'm a hack.

I can't stop myself from looking at the ghosts. I want to, but I can't. They're pushing something through, bringing it to me, sending it toward the stage.

I'm lost in this new choreography from the spirits, but I should keep talking. I've memorized my jokes back to front, so I should just fucking recite them and move on. *Stare at the ghosts and tell your damned jokes. Tell them. Mike. Please, damn it, tell them. Tell them now.*

"My mom keeps saying she wants grandkids. Won't stop busting my balls about it. 'When am I gonna be a grandmother? I want grandkids. Are you ever gonna have kids?'"

What are they pushing through? It's something big, something… It's a head. I can see hair. Brown, light brown.

"Mom. I have sex with anyone who lets me. I don't know what else I can do."

They're laughing. The crowd is laughing at my piece-of-shit jokes. Jokes about my mom. The head in the lights lifts, and as if my shitty joke summoned her, it's my mother.

Fuck.

"Mom."

I say that. I say it into the microphone as if it is a tag at the end of the punchline, and maybe it is, because my mother is dead, and all these people in the audience laughed at my joke mocking her. They don't know. They don't know she's dead. They laughed at my dead mother like sick assholes, and I'm the king of the sick assholes because I led them to that laugh. My mom is dead. That's the punchline. They just don't know that part of the joke.

She's looking at me.

I'm looking at her.

The audience is waiting.

My mother. Her face. People don't have one face; they have many. And if you study them, know them completely, you can use them as a timeline. This face, this one looking at me right now, it belongs to May 23rd, at around eleven o'clock.

The very last face she gave me.

She couldn't speak then, only grumbled in those last few days, moaned, made sounds of pain, but she spoke with that last look, with her eyes, and her scrunched nose, and her mouth agape. She told me so much.

There are people waiting for me. A crowd, an angry manager, the bartender, the other comics on the show. Eyes are on me, and I can't breathe. I'm sucking oxygen in, but nothing's coming out. No air. No words.

And my mother groans. It's so fucking loud.

I'm crying, but I'm talking. Maybe I am crying inside and holding it together for the audience. I'm talking, but I don't know what I am saying. Autopilot. Words are coming out and Jesus, I hope they're jokes. Setup, punchline, tag, tag, tag. I don't know, because I can't hear myself, can't even understand my own sentences.

The audience does. They must. They're laughing. I think they're laughing. It's so hard to tell.

Two conversations. One for the crowd, me the talker, them the listeners. One with my mom, neither of us saying a word.

It's all in the movements. It's our last conversation, the one we had while I propped her head up with my hand, her hot neck sweaty against my palm, and her breath pouring out like machine gun fire.

Her: *You need to fix this. You need to do things right. I can't die until I know you can do things right. Promise me. Promise me. Dear God, I can't take the pain anymore, but I can't leave until I know you can do things right. This pain. This is you. I would have left it a long time ago. I wouldn't be suffering. You're making me do this. Because I can't trust you. Because I can't know you'll be okay to take care of yourself.*

Me: *Mom, please, don't go. No, go. It's okay. You need to go. You need to stop suffering. I can do this. I'll be okay. I promise.*

Her: *You're lying.*

Me: *I AM lying. I am. I can't do this without you. I can't wake up tomorrow and live and walk and eat and know you aren't here. I can't. Stop suffering. Just stop. Wake up and tell me it's all a joke. It's just a joke. All of it. You're fine. I'm fine. We'll be fine. I promise.*

The crowd is dying. Cracking up. I hear claps with the laughs. That's always a good sign. Claps and laughs. Laughter is great. When it's small, it's like a burp, a strange, uncontrollable sound escaping you. When it gets more intense, it can hurt. You lose your breath. Your chest stings. Your abs tighten. It's painful to laugh like that. You cry, maybe. Your face flushes red. Maybe it's killing you, the laugh. The better the laugh, the higher the pitch. Sometimes it's so intense it can be mistaken for a scream. You know what I mean? When you hear that noise in the distance and you ask, "Is someone being killed? Do they need help?" They don't, you decide. You laugh at yourself because you were worried, and they were just enjoying life, just laughing. It's so hard to tell, isn't it? The sounds of intense enjoyment and agonizing pain. It doesn't take much for one to become the other.

And my mother, she's breathing so fast it's making my arms shake. She's dying in my arms, I know this, but she's forcing me to make a promise I can't keep. I can't, but I need to. For her. For once, I should do something for someone else.

The ghosts agree with this thought, because they spin in the light, tumbling, tossing.

No, they're pushing something else through, and I know what it is because it's that time. I remember the story. As I held my mother, as she died, as she furrowed her brow to say one last thing, it all halted, and Luna pushed his front paws up to my knees, trying to get in on the conversation.

And there he is just in time, in the light, the cloudy monsters swirling and presenting him to me. *Look at what you did*, they're saying.

I know! I know! I get it. The laughter died, so I might have actually said that into the microphone.

Luna. He's up, scooted onto my lap, between my arms as they prop my mother's head. And Luna and my mom make eye contact. My mother gives him a new look. This conversation isn't for me. It's for them, her and the dog.

Take care of him, my mother's expression asks the dog. She didn't ask me to take care of her dog, she asked her dog to take care of me.

And he did. He did. He came to me as I lay fetal in my bed, bawling, and he snuck his little head between my feet and curled up. He lay there, saying, *Let's make a deal. She's gone now, not coming back, and we need each other. We need to take care of each other.*

I'm so fucking sorry, Luna.

I definitely said that into the mic, because the crowd gasps, whispers.

And boom, the ghosts break free from the lights. They're diving into people, biting, clawing, ripping into the laughter. I can see all this behind Luna, but it's blurred. My focus remains on the dog.

I'm so sorry, Luna.

I took care of him. For a while, I did. He was my mother,

an extension of her, and I loved him for that, for keeping her with me in some small way.

Tables topple over, big booms with shattering glass. Swirls of mist float from person to person, drinks-a-flying, chaos, but I'm a statue on the stage.

Luna. Are you listening? Remember the time I hadn't eaten in two days, and I found the seven dollars in my winter coat, and I bought you food with it? I bought you food, because you mattered more than me. Remember that, Luna?

The manager yells to shut it down. "Shut it down." Those are his words. Is it me he wants to shut down? He can't possibly be talking about ghosts. What a crazy reaction to your club turning into a bloodbath. Shut it down?

Luna, I'm sorry. I know I messed up, but I tried, didn't I? I loved you. I know I slept too often, stopped taking you out. It was every other hour. Then it was every four. Then I would go whole days without taking you out and I wouldn't get mad at you for pissing and shitting on the kitchen floor. I cleaned it up, sometimes right away. It always got cleaned up, eventually.

The back door slams open, cracks against the outside stone wall. People are screaming, a horrific sound echoing through the room as the crisp night air seeps in. Chaos. Running, flailing, screaming.

But then I took you out, Luna. I took you out, and you betrayed me. You left me. You left me alone. You ran and ran, and by the time I realized you took off, I couldn't find you, and I looked everywhere. For days. I called out in the streets, and I put up signs, and I worried I'd find out you got hit by a car. It would have killed me. If a car hit you, I would have died, too.

But you didn't get hit by a car. You just left, because you had to. You tried. We had our agreement, and I let you down. I let you down.

The ghosts hit me. I fall, snap out of the memory. I'm back in the club, on the stage, lying on my back, and the ghosts are on top of me, holding me down, screaming at me, screaming, screaming, screaming. *You fuck. You fuck*, they are saying.

Luna, please.

Are you listening?

You.

Are you listening?

Luna.

Anyone.

Please.

Are you listening?

They rip the mic from me, rip it from my clenched hands.

Are you listening?

Are you listening?

I'm sorry.

Are you listening?

I wrote this story very shortly after I sobered up. A lot of it is true, but in a less dramatic fashion. I did inherit my mother's dog (her real name was Molly) and Molly did save me many nights when I didn't think I could pull through. I never treated her the way the narrator does in this story, but I recognized my own downfall and knew it wouldn't be long before I couldn't take care of the dog anymore. Molly didn't run away. Instead, I gave her to someone I knew could take better care of her than I could. I remember giving her a last hug before we parted, and the look in her eyes, those all-too-intelligent eyes, that understood what was happening. It was the kind of look that said, "I don't care how rough the road ahead is, I'd rather take it with you." And I wish I could have said, "Yes, please. Stay with me," but I knew in the long run, Molly would be happier in a better environment, and that proved true. She even had some doggie friends in her new home. And I am more than glad she didn't have to witness all that was to become of me in the years that followed.

NOW HIRING

Cassidy entered the lobby through the second set of double doors, Addie in tow, latched to her skirt by the forceful grip of an anxious five-year-old. As soon as the doors had swung open, a new leather smell wafted into Cassidy's nose. She scanned the Art Deco architecture around her and wondered how it was supposed to feel welcoming. The square shapes melding into bigger square shapes, and the bright lights, marble arches, sleek, shiny floors, all sent a cold disquiet down her spine. A showcase of opulence for opulence's sake.

She sat on a hard leather seat, and her daughter hoisted herself into the chair next to her. Addie's little legs dangled from the cartoonishly large leather monstrosity.

Cassidy rubbed the hem of her skirt between her thumb and index finger, and Addie noticed. The little girl extended her hand and wrapped her little fingers around her mom's sweaty palm.

"It's okay, Mama."

Cassidy released a ball of air from her throat. "I know, baby. These things always make me nervous, that's all."

She attempted to calm herself by examining the lobby

some more. For all its vastness, it lacked people. The only other person there besides Cassidy and Addie was a receptionist who hadn't looked up from a magazine, not even to greet Cassidy when she arrived. The phones weren't ringing. There was no hustle and bustle.

There were doors, tons of them. At least seven on the bottom floor, and more on the second story, which was just a long hallway wrapping around the outer walls in an open floor plan. Two staircases climbed to the lanky floor, so one could walk up, around, and back down in a matter of seconds. It was like a playground, except it never led to fun.

After a few moments, a door opened across from where Cassidy sat, and a handsome man stepped out. He wore a black suit jacket with a dark blue button-down under it. The outfit screamed, "I am powerful, please believe me."

He waltzed to the receptionist, put his hand on her shoulder, and whispered to her. As the woman responded, he nodded.

His smile was charming, and Cassidy had no doubt his bright blue eyes attracted many women, but his self-importance exuded from his mannerisms and leaked from his pores. She hated him, she knew, but told herself she'd try not to.

He stepped over to Cassidy with an arm drawn. "You must be Cassidy Daniels? I'm Roger. I'll be interviewing you today."

She stood up and shook his hand. "Yes, sir." She nodded toward Addie. "I'm sorry. Babysitter fell through, and while I know that's probably a poor reflection on our first meeting, I assure you it won't be a problem if I get the job."

He let go of her hand and smiled. "Not a problem at all. We are very child-friendly here. In fact, some of the other employees bring their children in regularly. I'll admit, it's not an ideal environment for them, gets a little boring, but it's not an issue on our end."

Cassidy tried to hide the excitement building inside her.

But if she could save money on sitters, the potential job just scored some major points.

"Come with me." He nodded toward the office and turned toward it.

Cassidy grabbed Addie's hand, and they walked behind Roger. As they approached the door, Roger did a double take on Addie.

"Oh, I'm sorry. Just you for this part."

Cassidy took a moment to register what he meant. "Oh, uh."

Roger read the hesitation on her face. "It's okay. Just stay here for a second."

He marched to the front double doors and pulled out a ring of keys. After he locked the doors, he pulled on them to showcase they weren't opening. "No one will be able to come in. And Kathy here will keep an eye on your daughter."

"It's just…" She wanted to say that Addie didn't do well alone, that she cried whenever left to her own devices, but knew that adding more problems to an already embarrassing start would only hurt her chances of getting the job.

Roger put his pointer finger up and moved past them into his office, where he lifted the shade on a large front window.

He came back out all smiles. "See, and now you can keep an eye on her the whole time."

"Okay," Cassidy said, still just as nervous about the prospects, but unwilling to push it.

She brought Addie back to her seat and took her tablet from her purse. "Here, you can play your Shimmer and Shine video game while I do the interview, okay?"

"And if you want to see your mommy, you can come peek through that window right there." Roger turned up his charming grin. It did nothing for Cassidy but worked wonders on Addie.

Addie took the tablet. "Good luck, Mommy." She went headfirst into her game.

"That's the spirit," Roger said and headed back to the office without a second glance.

Cassidy took a deep inhale and followed the man into the abyss, stopping once before entering to give a last safety check on her daughter. She slowly closed the door to the office, putting a final divider between her and her rock, the one person who gave her clarity and hope.

She sat down on another cold leather seat, an apparent staple of McCorrmick's Everywhere Inc., and forced a big, bright smile. "Sorry again for all of that. We've been in lockdown for the last year, so getting a new babysitter and preparing to go back out in the world had a few speed bumps."

Roger waved her comments away. "It's really understandable. No worries. So, let's begin, shall we?"

She nodded, shifted in her seat, and cleared her throat.

"Why do you want to work at McCorrmick's?"

I don't, she thought. *I'd like to stay home with my daughter, find something I can do from my computer, but I need an income now, and you're hiring.*

"Well, you're a fairly new company, which means I can join from the ground floor, but you've also proven yourself. During the pandemic, when everyone else was bleeding money and closing stores, you've expanded, and you're only growing by the day. I want to join the team, help the company grow further, and be a part of its success story."

Roger leaned back. "You've done your research on us, then?"

"Oh, yes. I didn't just apply randomly. I knew I wanted to be here." *And the lie detector determined that was a lie.* Cassidy stopped herself from giggling at her own thought.

Roger flipped through the pages of Cassidy's resume. He lifted his head to her and pressed his lips together. They stared at each other for a moment, her waiting for him to say something, him thinking of what to say. Cassidy placed her hands to the sides of her butt, nearly tucking them in, trying to quell the nervous shake building in her fingers.

Finally, the silence broke when Roger clapped his hands together so loudly, it sent Cassidy's heart into her brain.

"I guess that's all I have."

Cassidy's eyebrows sank. "That's it?"

Roger shrugged and put his hands up as if he were the lady of justice statue. "That's all I got."

For a moment, Cassidy convinced herself she had such an impressive resume, they didn't need to ask her more than one question, but she knew that wasn't the case. He asked one question so as not to waste any more time on someone he had no intention of hiring.

She refused to show him the defeat she felt, so she stood up, extended her hand for a shake, and with the bubbliest voice she could muster, said, "Thank you, sir. I look forward to hearing back from you."

He nodded, shook her hand, stood up, and walked her to the door.

When the door opened, Addie wasn't in her seat. Cassidy turned her head left and right, no Addie anywhere.

She ran to the seat, searching for the tablet. She turned to the receptionist, who stared blankly at a computer screen. "Where did she go? The bathroom?"

The receptionist looked up. "Who?"

"My daughter. She was sitting here. You were supposed to be watching her."

Roger tilted his head. "You had someone with you?"

Cassidy's knees buckled. All the air in her body vanished. "What the hell are you talking about? You just locked the front doors and opened your window shade and did this whole show. Where did she go?"

Roger stepped back. "I have no idea what you're talking about, but I didn't see you sitting with anyone."

Cassidy ran to the double doors and opened them.

Unlocked. She stretched out into the parking lot, leaning halfway out of the building. "Addie!" she shouted.

She ran back inside. "This isn't funny. Where did she go?"

Roger stepped toward her. "Ma'am. Let's calm down."

"Oh, fuck you. Don't tell me to calm down."

Some of the office doors on both floors opened, and heads peaked out, seeing what the commotion was about.

Roger waved to them all. "You can all return to work. I've got this under control."

Cassidy ran to the bathroom doors next to the receptionist —who stared in bewilderment.

"Addie," Cassidy yelled as she barged into the women's room, pushing through every stall door. "Addie, honey. Are you in here?"

Cassidy dashed back into the lobby, and as a new wave of panic and terror set in, she noticed the inane. She had been wrong about the architecture being Art Deco. It was like a grotesque version of Second Empire, but all wrong, horrid and jagged, sharp lines forcing themselves into each other. She waved the thought away and ran to the receptionist. Roger stood by the woman's desk, holding out his cell phone.

"I'm going to phone the police," he said as if it were a burden to him.

"Yes, do that. Immediately." Cassidy paced, chewing on the inside of her cheek. She thought about where she could check, where to look. Roger played dumb on the phone, telling the police he had no idea what was happening, but that a woman was saying her daughter was missing. Cassidy's first instinct was to run outside, but then she worried Addie would come out from under some nook in the office building, and her mom would be nowhere in sight.

She ran up the stairs.

"You can't just go up there," Roger yelled, following her with a quick gait. He held back from a full-on run, which Cassidy assumed had to do with his desire to keep up appearances. She was ruining the serenity of the office, creating an imperfect aura around the place.

"Addie!" she yelled as she marched down the hallway, peering into every room. When she passed an office with an ajar door, she pushed it open. Surprised employees sat behind their desks with bulging eyes, unsure what to do or say, or pretending to ignore the situation entirely, clicking endlessly on their mouses. Some of them had clients sitting on the opposite sides of their desks, and those clients did not hide the discomfort from their faces.

When she reached the end of the hall, she darted down the stairs, one big circle. Roger stayed a step behind.

"Listen, Miss Daniels, I don't fully understand what is happening here, but the police are on their way. Until they get here, can we just calm down? I promise you; no one has your daughter in their office."

She swung around, getting right in his face. "So, you admit I was here with my daughter?"

His head fell back an inch. "I don't know. I didn't see a child with you. That doesn't matter. If she is here, we will find her. The police will find her. But shouting from the rooftops won't change anything. If you did indeed bring your daughter with you, she would have heard you by now if she were in here. You wouldn't need to keep shouting. It's not that large of an office."

A loud squawk came from the front vestibule and the double doors opened. Two officers came through. One was a young gentleman. His scruffy blonde hair and thin frame made him look like a high schooler in a Halloween costume. The other officer, a muscular woman with a mouth full of gum, walked toward Cassidy and Roger with her hands on her waist.

The female officer wasted no time. "Are you the mother?" she asked.

"Yes, officer. Thank you so much for coming. Do you have people out there looking for her?"

"We have a car outside scanning the perimeter. I need more information from you." The woman ushered Cassidy to the lobby's leather seats while Roger moved toward the junior officer, who looked around the office with his arms folded over his chest as if he were cold and scared.

The female officer sat leaning in Cassidy's direction, getting close. She spoke with a calm voice, which did nothing to ease Cassidy's anxiety, but at least didn't add to it. "I need a description of your daughter."

Two more officers came through the double doors, both older gentlemen. The female officer turned to them. "Ah, would you guys do a quick scan of the place? Looking for a girl... How old?" She turned back to Cassidy.

"She's five," Cassidy shouted right to the men.

While they looked around, the female officer softened and offered Cassidy a smile. "I'm Officer Larring, and my partner over there is Officer Chase."

Officer Chase chatted with Roger, who was ushering the young officer to the receptionist's desk.

Cassidy stared at Officer Larring, not interested in formalities, but she soon realized the conversation was halted, waiting for her to identify herself. "I'm Cassidy."

Officer Larring shifted in her seat. Her walkie squawked, making Cassidy jolt, hoping it meant some sort of news on her daughter, but Larring ignored it, so Cassidy's hope deflated.

"Do you have any pictures of her on your phone that I can see?" Larring asked.

Cassidy took her phone out, and the screen came to life. Because of her nerves, she accidentally clicked on the camera app instead of photos, and she shook as she exited out. After tapping madly to get back to the home screen, her finger tapped on TikTok and a loud rap song blasted through the office, awakening the attention of Roger, the receptionist, and Officer Chase. Cassidy said, "Sorry," and they went back to their focus behind the desk. The receptionist clicked on her mouse, and they all stared at the computer screen.

Cassidy finally opened the photos app and scrolled through a grid of photos. As pictures flew down the screen, the month header changed from October to September to August. She shook her head, and reversed through the grid, going slower.

Where were the pictures of Addie in her new Disney Princess dresses? Where were the ones of Cassidy and Addie climbing trails in Arcadia? Her heart thumped hard in her chest, and the wetness in her mouth evaporated until it was hard to swallow.

"Sorry, I'm trying to find some."

She kept scrolling, the months changing to July and June. No pictures of her daughter. But then something else caught her attention, and she let out a deep groan. She had been so focused on finding pictures of Addie, that she failed to notice the contents she scrolled past.

Officer Chase called Larring over to whatever they were seeing on the computer at the receptionist's desk. Larring patted Cassidy's shoulder. "You keep searching. I will be right back."

Cassidy stared at the photos, horrified. They were her, but they weren't pictures of her life. She stood smiling at the camera with some other woman, younger, and beautiful. The woman almost resembled Cassidy when she was fifteen years younger. There were dozens of pictures of Cassidy with this woman. At a dance club, a Red Sox game, shopping. There were pictures of Cassidy with a man she'd never met but clearly acted as a boyfriend, based on the closeness and cutesiness of their photos together.

Was she going insane?

What the fuck was happening?

Her whole body trembled, and her muscles tensed so tightly, it made her stomach lurch and her spine ache.

"Cassidy, would you mind coming over here?" Larring asked.

Cassidy closed her phone and put it back in her purse. The world spun. The weird architecture turned to swirling Pollockesque color swatches. She floated to the receptionist's desk on wobbly legs.

"Are you sure you didn't leave Addie outside or in the car or something?" Officer Chase asked.

The other officers who had searched the building were all gathering now in the lobby, hovering a few feet away from the receptionist's desk, but leering up now and again to see what happened.

"No, I wouldn't leave a fucking five-year-old in the car."

"Come here. Look at this."

Roger and Officer Chase parted to give her room to see the computer screen. The receptionist hit a button, and the video of the lobby played. After a few seconds, Cassidy walked in playing on her phone. She giggled and waved to the receptionist, and then sat in the same seat she had sat in when she first entered the office. Tears formed in her eyes as she watched herself sitting in the chair, her legs crossed, the outer one bobbing up and down as she stayed face-first in the screen of her cell.

Roger came out of his office and shook her hand and the two of them went into his office. No Addie. Not once.

Cassidy cried, letting out sniffling whines. "No. No. No." She scanned the room, all eyes on her. "I'm not fucking crazy."

Larring put her arm on Cassidy's again, but it was starting to feel less comforting and more condescending. "No one thinks you're crazy. We think you had a stressful day. I would like you to come with me to the station so you can talk to a detective who is much better at asking the right questions and finding people. Meanwhile…" she ducked down an inch, so her eyes were level with Cassidy, "…I'm not giving up the search. We will have people checking all over the area, and when they find your daughter, they will bring her right to you."

"They did something. They fucked with my phone and messed up my photos and screwed with the videos. They did this." But she had no fight. The more she talked, the more illogical and insane she sounded. Her only hope was to speak with this detective. Maybe he could get the tapes and see if they had been tampered with. They must have the technology to do that, right?

***

She sat in a cold room, waiting for the detective. It was an interrogation room, which brought a new level of panic to Cassidy's gut. She wondered how many people sat in the same chair waiting for a question that would give them away. The misfiring nerves in her body caused trembling fingers and legs as if she were a criminal dreading the Inquisition.

The wait was unbearably long, and every ticking second from the wall clock felt like another mile away from her child. She imagined every worst-case scenario: abduction, trafficking, assault, death.

When the detective came in, his entire look set her at ease. If she were expecting Stabler, this man wasn't it. He looked twenty years past retirement, but sharp, astute. A paunchy belly protruded over his belt, where his flannel shirt tucked into his pants. Grandfatherly, she thought.

He looked like a caring grandpa.

The man sat across from her and fidgeted with a file. He appeared more nervous than she was.

"Miss Daniels, I'm Detective Billings, but you can call me Joe." He looked up from his file and gave her a friendly smile.

"Okay. Are they still looking for Addie?"

"Well, this is where I'm confused. Addie's not missing."

Cassidy's back straightened and a moan left her throat. "You found her?"

The detective put his hand up as if to say, "Halt."

He slapped the file's bottom edge against the table to even out the loose papers inside. "Addie is your only child, correct? You don't have two daughters with the same name?"

Her jaw slackened. "No?"

Suddenly, the irrational anxiety of sitting in the interrogation seat felt less ridiculous after all. Her body grew unbearably hot and sweat built on the base of her temples.

Detective Billings slid the file to her. "I'm just confused as to why you think your daughter is five. Addison Daniels, your child, is 19 years old. After I looked that up, I searched for her on Google and found her social media accounts. Most of them aren't private. Looks like she's a student at RISD. I found no other information of you having another child, but I did find your social accounts, and your Facebook profile picture is you with Addie, from the looks of it."

Cassidy nearly threw up as her stomach lurched into her chest. She released the pressure with a low groan and a full purging of her frustrations and horror by unleashing her tears in a torrent.

"This is crazy. This is so fucking crazy. How are they doing this? How is this possible?"

She flipped the file open and saw photocopies of Addie's birth certificate, along with printed photos from her social media accounts. On the last page, she found an article about a fellowship award granted to Addison Daniels for outstanding achievement in something. It was hard to tell, too difficult to focus on reading it. On any other day, she would have loved the opportunity to see a glimpse at the wonders waiting in Addie's future, but on this day, her daughter was alone, gone, and no one believed she even existed as she truly had.

The detective said nothing while Cassidy bawled and flipped through the pages. She eventually closed the file, and the two sat in silence while Cassidy's cries settled down.

"Listen to me. I know this sounds crazy, but this isn't right. None of it. Addie is five. I brought her with me today to that job interview." But Cassidy's argument was thin against the depths of proof mounting against her. Video cameras, her own photos, birth certificates. Was it possible her mind broke and forgot the last 14 years?

The officer shrugged and pointed to the files. "Ma'am, I can only go by what I have."

She wiped her face, and asked, "Can I go outside and have a cigarette?"

The detective sighed. "Of course. You're not in trouble, Miss Daniels. I think you need to speak to a doctor. I'll have an officer escort you outside. You're not in custody, but I think you should come back inside so we can figure out what's going on here and see if we can help. I called your daughter's cell phone and left a message. I'll let you know as soon as she calls back so you can know she's safe."

Outside, Cassidy sat on a bench while a tall officer stood next to her with his hands cupped together over his waist. As she inhaled her cigarette, she opened her phone and scrolled through her photos. The mid-afternoon sun gave way to a thin stream of gray, and a light rain dripped from the heavens while Cassidy cried over pictures of her and a daughter that wasn't hers. They looked happy, this version of Cassidy and Addie, and seemed to enjoy each other's company. She hoped when her daughter grew up, they held a similar relationship.

If they ever found her.

She whimpered and sniffled, staring at this beautiful relationship unfold as the days and weeks changed on the screen. Raindrops formed little bubbles against the white borders and made it more difficult to dive deeper into the photos. As she swiped down, the screen jittered and bounced. She clicked the side of her cell and the wonderful life not hers turned to dark black.

One more inhale, and she stubbed her cigarette on the top of the ashtray pole before pushing the butt into the receptacle.

Back inside, the officer ushered her into the interrogation room. Her wait was shorter this time. Detective Billings came in, sat across from her, crossed his arms over his chest, and sighed. "So, what's going on Cassidy? What's happening?"

She noticed he avoided outright accusing her of lying or being wacked out of her mind. He didn't lay any blame on her for wasting police resources.

She debated what to say. Nothing seemed adequate to explain her horror. No amount of pleading could battle against records, video recordings, and photos. None of it made sense, and Cassidy no longer understood how deep this conspiracy was, or whether she truly had gone mad.

Billings tried again. "Tell me what you're thinking."

She opened her mouth to speak, but all she could muster was another groan.

He tapped the table. "I'm going to have someone else come in and speak to you."

He stood up and left. She expected a shrink to enter at any point. Despite the nerves, and the concern for her child, a sleepiness clouded over her. Time ticked by in a slow crawl, minutes, half an hour, an hour. Waiting and waiting. Panic turned to madness. She wanted out. Wanted to run until she dropped and woke up back in the real world. She rested her head on the table, and her eyelids weighed down, down, down, until everything turned black.

***

She woke up to a cell phone ringtone playing. Her eyes opened slowly, and disbelief washed over her. Were the lights off? Did they just let her sleep? The familiar smell of her dusty afghan took hold. Addie had wiped her hands on it after numerous peanut butter and jellies, and no matter how many times Cassidy had washed it, the slight smell of peanut butter lingered, mixing with the musty smell of the old blanket.

Sure enough, her fingers slipped into the patterned holes. She was home, but that didn't make sense. How did she get here? Was her memory going completely, or had she just had the world's most visceral and horrible dream?

With half-awake movements, she fumbled for the phone, playing a tune she didn't recognize, and checked the screen. Addie was calling, and the photo showing on the screen was the same adult version of her daughter she had seen in her photos earlier.

She picked up the phone and said, "Hello," trying to hide the sadness in her voice.

"Mom? What's going on? Some detective called me."

Cassidy sat up, her feet dangling from the bed. "Addie?"

"Yeah. Mom, is everything okay?"

She cried now, unable to pull back the tears.

"Mom, what's happening? Are you okay?"

"Addie, have you had a good life?"

There was a pause, and it broke her heart. Addie sighed.

"Why do you always do this?"

"Do what?" She stepped off the bed, moving in the pitch blackness only broken by the bright screen against her face.

"It's fine, Mom. You're fine. You did your best."

"What does that mean?"

Addie sighed again, this time more dramatically. "You always need to prove something to yourself. Every time I visit, you take a thousand pictures and post them on Facebook, talking about us being best friends. You're obviously trying to convince yourself of something, but whatever it is, I don't blame you. You have nothing to prove to me. You worked all the time. I get it. You had to keep us alive."

She shook her head as if Addie could see her. "I don't know what that means. Any of this."

"Mama?"

Cassidy screamed and threw the phone down as if it were attacking her. The word "Mama" came from the other room, from the voice of Addie. Her Addie. The Addie who marched around the house singing Disney Princess songs, who always ate French toast for breakfast, and who refused to sit down in the bath. Her Addie. So, who the fuck was on the phone?

"Addie?"

The voice on the phone called to her, but she could no longer make out the words. She turned the corner into the hallway of their apartment and saw the silhouette of her daughter standing in the center.

"Mama? What's wrong?"

Since Addie had gone missing, all Cassidy could think about was hugging her daughter, but now that Addie stood in front of her in the darkness, she feared touching her, worried that any connection would disrupt the laws of the world, and it would all fracture and disappear.

Addie turned around, walking down the hall to the living room. "Come on. Let's watch something."

As she walked, Cassidy recognized something off about her daughter. She walked slanted, as if she were a shadow bending from the direction of the sun. And now that Cassidy thought about it, Addie's voice was different, too. Sing-songy. Higher than normal.

"Mama. Come."

Nothing felt right, yet Cassidy stepped forward, following wherever Addie went. Her daughter sat on the couch, and slapped the seat next to her, calling her mother over. Even with the moonlight slicing through the blinds, Cassidy couldn't make out Addie's facial features, and a desire to see those soft details struck her gut like a right hook. She needed to see

Addie's heart shaped nose, the deep indent of her philtrum, her droopy brown eyes.

As if Addie knew these thoughts and wanted to play, she put her head down into her chest.

Cassidy sat next to her, wanting to squeeze her so tightly it merged them together, but she was also still too scared to touch her.

The house phone rang a loud shrill ring. Cassidy screamed at the unexpected sound. No one ever called on that phone. She only had it because it was easier for Addie to call 911 if needed, so she had taken her mother's old-school phone with the answering machine. She glanced at the time on the cable box. 3:17. Who the hell would be calling in the middle of the night? Maybe adult Addie, or the police. She put her arm around her real daughter, finally touching her, and the world didn't break in half. Instead, Addie rested her head against her mother's side, and everything slipped into place. For two seconds, the world had righted itself.

The phone stopped ringing, and Cassidy's annoying voice came on the old answering machine. "This is Cass and Ads, tell me what ya got?"

The fuzzy sound of the answering machine felt heavy in the otherwise silent air. Then, Roger's voice came on.

"Hey, Cassidy, we just wanted to let you know we were all inspired by your interview today, and we want to get you training on Monday. Please give me a call back to confirm, and otherwise, we will see you then. Oh, and congrats."

What.

The.

Fuck.

We were inspired?

Inspired?

It's fucking three in the morning.

Hired?

"Congrats, Mommy." Addie pressed her head deeper into

Cassidy's side. So deeply, Cassidy tilted sideways. Addie turned her face so that her hot breath slapped against the bare skin on Cassidy's arm.

"Congrats," she said again with a muffled voice thanks to her mouth pressing against her mom's flesh.

"Congrats."

And she bit.

Cassidy screamed and yanked her arm away. She stood up, shocked, confused.

Blood oozed down her arm, a big chunk of skin missing. Addie spit it out onto the floor and giggled.

"What's happening, Mom?" She slipped to the floor and flailed as if having a seizure. Cracking sounds filled the room as Addie's limbs stretched and her skin ripped from the sudden new growth.

Cassidy screamed.

Exposed bone and muscle twitched and pulsed. Addie made a low continuous grumble that melded in Cassidy's brain to the sound of a popcorn bag popping. All of Addie's limbs tightened, bent, and stretched. Ripping.

Cassidy closed her eyes, but she betrayed herself, prying them open, needing to see the horror, the insanity. She backed against the wall, smacking her head into a picture frame. The room spun, and she bit back a tidal wave of vomit.

Addie screamed in pain, writhing all over the floor. "Mama, help me!"

Cassidy put her arm forward, but kept herself against the wall, hoping the simple feeling of the smooth surface would plant her on Earth and not in the strange delusional galaxy she had clearly slipped into.

"Mama." Addie's jaw opened and cracked, breaking free from her face. Her skin began to move like worms lived under it, and it reattached itself to the places it had separated, then it wrinkled and formed flaps and flabs.

Cassidy fell, her back sliding down the wall until her butt

hit the floor, her knees bent in front of her. Her breath wouldn't come to her, stuck lodged in her lungs.

"Mama, help me."

Addie flipped to her side and stared directly at Cassidy, and for the first time, her features came into view. They were Addie's features but all wrong, crooked, angled slightly off, and her skin had spots and sores. She had turned into a horrific version of the adult Addie in Cassidy's cell phone pictures.

Addie's arm swung over her body, and her hand slammed into the floorboards. She used the blood-soaked hand to drag her body closer to her mother, and Cassidy shivered.

"Mama." The voice no longer sounded like Addie. Now it was more like a grotesque gurgle.

"Mama."

Slap. She slid closer.

Slap.

Goose pimples crawled up Cassidy's arms. She stood to run, but her body fought against her, freezing her in place until she slid back down.

Slap.

Addie crept her face up her mother's leg, and the weight of her body rested on Cassidy's knees, causing them to unbend.

Slap, right at Cassidy's side.

"Con."

Addie's face drove into Cassidy's belly.

"Grats."

She bit, ripping the flesh around Cassidy's belly button. Cassidy screamed.

Addie bit again, and her fingers dug into her mother's neck.

Cassidy dug her own fingertips into her palms and let her daughter feast on her. The skin snapped off her body into her daughter's hungry maw, the pain of each bite drilling into Cassidy's skull.

Addie chewed on the meaty pieces and spit them out, and Cassidy did nothing to fight, only winced in pain and anguish.

As Addie continued to eat, Cassidy stopped screaming, and the only sounds that filled the room were the loud smacks of her daughter's chewing, and her other daughter on the phone, yelling, "It's okay, Mama!"

I wrote this story right as everyone returned to work after the pandemic. It wasn't a statement on working or staying home, but I saw a lot of commentary on social media where folks called other people lazy for continuing to stay home for as long as they were allowed. And I thought about the single moms and dads who work their asses off all day at two jobs to provide for the children they never get to spend time with, and I understood why they wanted to eke out as much of that time at home as possible. This story puts Cassidy in a position where she finds what looks like a good job, and in an instant, her child is no longer hers. Years have passed in her daughter's life, and Cassidy missed it all. I didn't want to condemn the idea of working, and that's why Addie tells her mom on the phone that she understood her mother needed to work to provide for them, and from the pictures on the phone and the way the two women talk, it sounds like they both managed to find happiness. Still, I wish they got more of that time together. Meanwhile, at the end, Cassidy gets to see her daughter young again. She gets, for a brief moment, to cling to that, but then the job offer is extended, and her daughter grows older right in front of her eyes, and that ends up literally eating her alive.

THE DUNES

We were barreling by the fields
Dust-kissed, and anxious.
By the church with the neon cross
Brightly lit at midnight.
She was blue haired
Windswept and fresh out of smokes.
I was in love
With a permanence only kids believe in.
But we thinned out, as these things go
Like water dripping through the cracks of my fingers
Until we are empty.
She said, "Let's roll down the dunes."
So, we die on hills we can't stand on
And laugh little nightmares
To the bold black night.
And if we chose to listen,
We'd hear it laugh back.

I AM NOT ME ANYMORE

THE FOLLOWING TRANSCRIPT COMES FROM A VOICE RECORDER APP ON CHRIS MCDONALD'S IPHONE, DATED 08/08/23. THE FIRST RECORDING STARTED AT 5:45 PM:

I am not me anymore. The truth is I haven't been in quite some time, but I'm only realizing the depths of it now, as I sit in traffic on 95. Please, Julia, understand one thing. This isn't some way-too-early midlife crisis. It's not about you. It's not about work. This isn't some deep-seated desire to break free and do something drastic, although something drastic is about to happen, which I guess is why I clicked the recorder app and hit play. I need this to go forward, and for you to hear it all, because it's going to be fucking insane and I know it's insane, and nothing will happen like it should and when I get home two hours or three hours or four days late from work and you're wondering what the fuck I was doing and thinking, I'll have this recording for as long as the battery lasts and you'll understand the thought process behind my weird actions.

Fuck. I should back up. So, as I said, I'm sitting in traffic on 95. It was a good day at work, everything went well. Jason asked if we could have dinner with him and Jenna this weekend. I said probably. I know how you like to plan spur-of-the-moment hikes on Saturday, so I didn't want to commit without chatting with you.

Anyway, it's 5:45 now, and traffic is rough. Hardly moving forward at all. There's a giant red truck in front of me with plywood stacked and hanging over the tailgate. It's the most slipshod job I've ever seen, the planks zigging and zagging off each other like latticework drawn by a child.

It got me thinking of that infamous scene from one of the *Final Destination* sequels. Don't worry, these are thin wooden pieces, so they wouldn't fly through the windshield and sever my head or anything, but it just got me thinking about it, which got me thinking about death. Ya know?

I've been stuck deadlocked about ten feet in front of the bridge that carries Park Ave over 95. I used to walk that bridge every single day on my way home from Cranston East. I remember holding hands with Tiffany, which I know you don't want to hear about, but I just remembered it because of the bridge, how we'd always hold hands walking across it. I remember Corey and I dribbling a basketball on our way to the Park View courts, which I didn't even think at the time was weird. Doric was way closer. Why didn't Corey and I play at Doric? Well, now it's coming to me.

SIGHING

That bridge. I used to cross it all the time. And of course, that got me thinking about the other bridge. The bridge that brought all of this into my brain.

LAUGHTER

Jesus, what an asshole I am. I get stuck under this fucking bridge every damned day, and only today do I realize how much my life has been shaped by the day we crossed the other bridge. Maybe I'm not an asshole. I don't think I've been in control of my thoughts. Or even my emotions.

Look, I need to back up again. I know this is getting weird. Julia, the most important thing you need to understand in all of this is I am happy. Truly. I'm always happy. With you. With life. But see, that's the problem. I'm always happy. I'm never angry, or sad, or haunted. It's not a good way to live, to miss out on those things, especially with the baggage I carry. The secrets. I need you to know those secrets, and I need to tell them as I'm doing all of this, but I also need to remind myself of all of it, so that's why I'm recording. Because you're coming with me on a trip. And for the first time since I was thirteen, I'm terrified. Don't get me wrong, I've been scared. A little. For crying out loud, about two weeks ago, a semi was driving on the wrong side of 95 on my way into work, and I just went about my day. The thing was barreling too. Cars were shifting lanes without paying attention just to get out of the way of this thing. Better to sideswipe another car than to meet face-first with a semi. I was scared when that happened. But I wasn't terrified. Not like this. And my adrenaline quelled five minutes later. You have to see something wrong with that, right? That's insane, to stabilize so quickly. It's insane because it's not real. I'm not real.

I know that's hard to hear and to understand right now, but the me you know isn't really me. Whatever has been there, keeping me in my lane, it's breaking. I'm breaking, and in this case, it's a good thing. Truth be told, I think I always knew something was wrong. No, you know what? I'm sure of it. I always was. Jesse is the perfect example! I'll talk more about him later, but he's my proof I knew something was wrong, because every time I talked to him, my hairs stood on end, and my brain shot these like, weird alerts at me. And I kept that kind of thing to myself because it just seemed like one of those stupid reactions people have to each other sometimes, but now it's all filling in, this picture. It's piecing together. I guess right now it's like the wood pieces in front of me, all crisscrossed and mangled, but I'm going to hammer that shit together and make sense of it all.

I wish this clicked before now, because the next exit isn't

until Jefferson Boulevard, which means I'll have to do some driving to get back to where I need to be. It's not far, but if I want to do this right, I need to start where we started, my friends and me. I need to follow the ritual.

LAUGHTER

Ritual? If I didn't sound crazy before, I know I do now. I don't mean a ritual. We all hung out every day, and we had all sorts of adventures. We didn't do the ritual every day, or even most days. And it's not like we called it a ritual, or planned to keep the system in place, it's just how it worked out. Whenever we went to Doric for a pickup touch football game, we did the same three things after. Every time. I don't know why. It's just how it worked.

After the incident, we didn't just break one piece of the pattern. We stopped them all.

It's worse than that because it would make sense for us to stop doing all that stuff after what happened to us. But we didn't just quit the ritual, we quit remembering the ritual. We quit remembering each other. We quit all of it. I wonder if I called Jesse right now and told him all of this, would he think I was crazy, or would his brain start to break free from the thing living inside us? Would he know? Jesus. Did any of them remember, even a sliver of it? Did it come back to some of them before they died?

INAUDIBLE

I don't know how well this recorder works, if you can hear the blinker clicking, but I'm officially moving over a lane, and that may not seem like a big deal, but it's the first time I've broken my routine in forever. As I shifted over to the right, I knew I wasn't going to turn back from this. I'm getting off the exit onto Jefferson Boulevard, and I'm heading back to Cranston, and I'm going to my past life.

INAUDIBLE

I'm crying. I've never felt like this before. I guess you don't need to hear me sit in traffic. I'll start a new recording when I get closer to Doric, or if I think of something else to say. I know this all doesn't make a lot of sense right now, and it would be better if I just explained it all, but A.) I don't know it all yet. My mind is slowly pulling it in, but as for now, it's just not clear enough, and B.) We're going to the tracks, and that's where all the answers are, where it all happened, and I think it would be best to explain it where it happened, where I can visualize it. It'll be clearer that way. For both of us.

INAUDIBLE

THE FOLLOWING ENTRY COMES FROM WILLIAM HUFFMAN'S DIARY, DATED 09/05/2009:

The wake was bullshit. So many kids Matt hated pretending they were best friends. I fucking hate that. They're literally using his death for sympathy. Fuck them. It was weird to see him in the casket. I cried, but it wasn't just because of him. I feel like I was always the little brother tugging behind him, attached by a cord that he dragged. And now he's dead. I feel doomed. Like I'm going next, and I'm going soon. He's still pulling that cord. I'm as good as gone.

THE FOLLOWING TRANSCRIPT COMES FROM A VOICE RECORDER APP ON CHRIS MCDONALD'S IPHONE, DATED 08/08/23. THIS SECOND RECORDING STARTED AT 6:22 PM:

Okay, I'm at Doric field now. We'd all meet up by the bowling alley on Park Ave. Sometimes we'd go behind it and share a cigarette Pete would steal from his dad. If we had markers, we'd write our names on the wall. The wall is cement, all bumpy and rough, so the tags always looked like shit. Not that we were any good at it to begin with. I went there to check it out, but they painted over the wall, so none of our graffiti was there anymore. I would have recorded something, but it felt empty. I don't remember anything strange happening until we hit Doric.

Okay, so the first thing I have to explain is our group of friends hovered around twenty people. Different people hung out on different days, but we only played football at Doric when it was the exact right six people. I don't know. A couple of friends just didn't play. Ben and his brother, Chad, were just cheating fucks at everything they played. Bix loved to play, but he sucked, and he was short. We always worried we'd break him. I mean, we were all scrawny kids, but Bix was next-level little.

It had to be me, Corey, Jesse, Billy, Matt, and Pete. Always. And it couldn't be less. If one of us couldn't play, none of us played. With five people, one person had to be QB for both sides, and someone always accused that person of going extra for one side. Favoritism. And if we only had four people, it just wasn't as fun as it was with two wide receivers on both teams.

It had to be six, and it had to us six.

I know this is probably boring the shit out of you because you don't like football, but it's important to the story because that day, we broke our own unspoken rule. There were only five of us.

INAUDIBLE

LOUD SIGHING

Like a week before, Matt had died. He got hit by a car running across Park Ave. I walked by two hours after he got hit. It was all cleaned up and cars were driving by like nothing had happened, but his shoe… One of his shoes was just chilling by the drain on the sidewalk. I knew it was his because he was a goof and wore these boat shoes that were red on one side and white on the other. So weird looking.

Anyway, we were all pretty fucked up about it, but Billy was his little brother, and he was really fucked up, just a shell of himself. At the wake, he was like comatose, wouldn't respond to anything, just stared off into space with tears coming down his face in an endless stream. I'd never seen anyone like that before or since. He was in another world.

We were dumb kids, didn't know how to make someone feel better. In hindsight, dragging him to mimic the fun and games we usually had with his now-deceased brother was probably a shit idea, but at the time it made sense. We thought we'd cheer him up by going through the ritual. Remember, we didn't actually call it that.

Now, the football and all the other bullshit we knew wouldn't help. It was the end part we thought would help him feel better, but like I said, if we were going to do one, we had to do it all. It was always the same way. Always.

So, we played football, and it was fun for a bit. Billy even seemed to get into it. When he was on fire… Man, he was a good receiver. Fast, nimble. He could go a million miles an hour and then just dead stop and spin for a catch. It was inhuman.

I think it was Corey who noticed the sound first. He was sensitive to shit. The kind of kid who was always sick, always complaining. We're mid-game, playing to ten touchdowns, and Corey's like, "We should leave. I want to leave."

And we were all like, "What the fuck are you talking about? We're having fun." And all of us are looking at Billy, who is actually smiling and goofing with Pete. I thought Corey was going to bitch about me being QB. Like I said, someone always accused the designated QB of favoring one team, and Corey and Jesse were currently losing to Billy and Pete.

But then Corey asks us if we can hear the noise. I didn't hear it. I thought he was bullshitting, trying to find a way out of the game he was losing. But then Billy nodded. His eyes were getting watery. He's like, "I hear it. I hear it. I can't believe you can hear it too. It's been driving me crazy since we started playing, but I didn't want to say anything."

Corey said something about it being so soft but so painful, and Billy got really excited about that, because that description let him know Corey was indeed hearing the same noise. The rest of us looked at them like they were crazy, but then

Pete goes, "Oh shit. What the fuck?" And he covers his ears, bending over like someone punched him in the gut.

I thought he was fucking around. No one likes to be left out, even when it's suffering they're missing out on. You see it all the time. When something terrible happens, everyone wants to chime in with a story about their proximity to the tragedy. We'd rather bleed together than smile alone.

But then Jesse growled. He shakes his head like an angry dog chewing on a rabbit. "Get it out. Get it out." He kept saying that. "Get it out." Then I knew none of them were faking, because Jesse never went along with shit. He was such an obstinate fucker. He'd go against the grain just to piss everyone off. If we all liked Ninja Turtles, he liked Barbies, and he'd kick anyone's ass who tried to mouth off about that. He'd never go along with something. In fact, he'd be the type to pretend he didn't hear it if he actually was.

My eyes grew to the size of saucers, just staring at my friends all screaming, hollering, complaining. Then it came to me. Slowly. At first, it was just a light ringing, like the sound a TV makes for a few seconds after you turn it off. But it ticked up a few notches every few seconds. It never got loud, but it got deeper into my skull. Imagine hearing a hurricane warning siren, but it's really far away, so you can only hear it a little. Now imagine it's not far away. It's inside your brain. Doesn't matter if it's loud, it's just too close. It's part of you.

I didn't react, didn't complain or holler like the rest of them. I was too scared. What could make five different people hear noises inside their heads? What could do that?

Billy put his hand on my shoulder, and we looked at each other for a few seconds. Finally, he said, "It's the field. We should leave."

Even then, even as the noise was assaulting us, I didn't want to leave, partly because I wanted to complete the game for Billy, but also it unnerved me to break the ritual. Maybe the noise was a result of us messing with it in the first place.

Maybe the ritual should have died with Matt. Well, hindsight now. We definitely should have let it die with Matt.

INAUDIBLE

A SHORT PERIOD OF SILENCE

Anyway, we listened to Billy and took off. As soon as our feet left the grass and hit the white cement sidewalk, we stopped hearing it. I wish now that I stepped back on the grass to see if it came back, but none of us tried that. We just left for the next part of the ritual.

As we walked down the sidewalk, we didn't bring it up. Like, we all just heard the same noise in our heads, and none of us thought about it again as soon as we left. You'd think a bunch of kids wouldn't shut up about a thing like that. But we just carried on like we had finished the football game as normal. I can't even remember thinking about that sound again until now, until I started telling the story.

A SHORT PERIOD OF SILENCE

I guess that's it for now. I'll make another recording when I get to the next place.

THE FOLLOWING IS A POEM WRITTEN BY COREY GEORGE, SUBMITTED TO THE PARK VIEW MIDDLE SCHOOL YOUNG POETS MAGAZINE ON 10/13/09. IT WAS NOT ACCEPTED, AND SCHOOL PSYCHOLOGISTS WERE CALLED TO SPEAK WITH HIM:

It disappeared for them when we stepped off the field.
Mine never went away.
Never.
Outside my head, the world keeps spinning.
Tomorrow comes with a flash from the sun.
My head never wakes up. Never slept in the first place.
Emptiness.
All I have left.
Nothing.

You can leave me here.
My mind is not my own.
Oh, God, it won't stop.
Run.
Everyone.

THE FOLLOWING IS A TRANSCRIPT FROM AN INTERVIEW WITH JESSE CAPALDI WITH THE WARWICK POLICE DEPARTMENT ON 09/03/23:

OFFICER DUCHANE: Want anything to drink?

JESSE CAPALDI: I'm good. Am I in trouble?

OFFICER DUCHANE: No. Not at all.

JESSE CAPALDI: It's not every day the police escort you outta work to ask you questions.

OFFICER FAZZIO: Sorry for the dramatics. We just need some info you might be able to help us with. It's no big deal.

OFFICER DUCHANE: Do you know what this might be about?

SILENCE

JESSE CAPALDI: Chris McDonald?

SILENCE

OFFICER FAZZIO: That's part of it. Did he call you a couple of weeks ago?

OFFICER DUCHANE: Specifically on August 8th?

JESSE CAPALDI: He did.

OFFICER DUCHANE: Can you tell us the nature of that phone call?

JESSE CAPALDI: I'd rather not.

SOMEONE SIGHING

OFFICER DUCHANE: Was it about Billy Hannah?

SILENCE

OFFICER DUCHANE: Jesse?

JESSE CAPALDI: It was.

PAPERS RUSTLING

OFFICER FAZZIO: Jesse, in 2009, you told the police Billy Hannah ran into the woods and you never saw him again. Is that a story you maintain today?

SILENCE

OFFICER DUCHANE: Jesse?

SILENCE

OFFICER DUCHANE: Jesse, can you answer the question?

JESSE CAPALDI: I'd rather not answer.

SOMEONE SIGHING

OFFICER FAZZIO: Let's step back a little. In a recording we obtained from Chris's iPhone, he mentioned a sound you all heard when you were playing football earlier that day. Do you remember hearing a weird sound?

SNIFFLING

OFFICER DUCHANE (WHISPERING): Get him a water.

JESSE CAPALDI: I don't need one.

OFFICER DUCHANE: You look upset. Do you need a few minutes?

JESSE CAPALDI: No.

OFFICER FAZZIO: Okay. Can you answer the question? Do you remember hearing a weird sound?

JESSE CAPALDI: Yes.

OFFICER DUCHANE: Why didn't you ever talk about hearing the sound before?

JESSE CAPALDI: I don't know.

OFFICER FAZZIO: Probably just didn't think it was important, right? What's a sound got to do with your missing friend, right?

JESSE CAPALDI: It wasn't that.

OFFICER DUCHANE: Then what was it?

JESSE CAPALDI: I just forgot all about it.

OFFICER DUCHANE: You forgot about it? Chris talked

about it like it was a hard thing to forget. I mean, he also mentioned forgetting it, but that seems strange, no?

JESSE CAPALDI: My mind kind of forgot everything about that day.

OFFICER FAZZIO: So, when did you remember it?

JESSE CAPALDI: When Chris called me.

OFFICER FAZZIO: So, you guys talked about that noise?

JESSE CAPALDI: No.

OFFICER DUCHANE: Then why did your conversation with him help you remember it?

JESSE CAPALDI: Because I haven't stopped hearing it since.

THE FOLLOWING TRANSCRIPT COMES FROM A VOICE RECORDER APP ON CHRIS MCDONALD'S IPHONE, DATED 08/08/23. THIS THIRD RECORDING STARTED AT 6:40 PM:

After the football game, we went to Chrissy Hester's house. This part of our routine started by accident. The first time we all played football together, we were headed to a different part of what became the ritual, but on the way, Chrissy was outside, sitting on her front steps, listening to music and smoking a cigarette. She had her computer at the window, speakers on the steps, wires snaking from them to the monitor. Weird times. It was probably all MP3s downloaded from Apple Music.

She listened to emo, which we all kind of liked, but we weren't cool, so we just liked the popular ones. The Used. Panic! At the Disco. Paramore. Would you call Paramore emo? See, I'm still so uncool. Anyway, she listened to bands like Atreyu, The Forecast, June, Thursday. They weren't like super underground or anything, but they seemed it to us.

We all had a crush on her. She was two years older, had that punk attitude, but also had her shit together. She was too good for us, so the fact she stopped us on that first go-around to chat was a miracle. We all sat on her stoop, and it was weirdly cool. Not awkward like you'd expect. She had a way of relaxing us, despite our obvious nerdiness and desperation.

Pete really had a thing for her, but he was a nervous kid, too nervous to even flirt. Jesse had no problem with it. He was always trying to impress her, but he didn't know anything about what girls liked. She liked music, not sports, yet he kept trying to brag about all his accomplishments with our pointless tag football games. Why do people always do that? Brag about something only they care about? Why don't they pay attention to what the other person likes? Seems like a good way to tell someone their needs and wants don't matter as much as yours.

We hung out that first time until the sky turned purple. Next time we played football, we expected to walk right by, but there she was again, hanging on her steps, and minutes later, there we were, drooling over her and her cool music tastes.

Even after two times, no one expected it to become a part of the ritual, but four or five times later, we ended up on her steps every time. Turns out that's pretty much all Chrissy did. Hung out on her porch and listened to music.

But on this day, the one where we all fled the field because of the noise in our brains, she wasn't there. Something about seeing those empty steps punched me in the guts harder than that eerie noise did. It was haunting. Empty space always is, but even more so when it had normally been filled by a friend.

We debated on what to do. Most of us just presumed we should move on, not thinking we were cool enough to knock on her door. Talking to the princess when she runs away into the woods isn't the same as rapping on the castle doors.

Surprisingly, Jesse and Pete, who had spent countless hours arguing over who would date her, didn't put up a fight. It was Billy who insisted we stop and knock. He said he felt weird moving on when we never had before. I don't know about the rest of the guys, but his usage of the words "moving on" crept up my spine and forced me to agree.

None of us put up a fight after that. Together, we stood on her steps and knocked. Together, we waited. Together, we felt the weight of the darkness in her windows and worried what yet another change to our routine would mean. I think at this point, I started to sense an impending doom on our day, God's finger pressing us into the cement. We were in for trouble, but I didn't know what kind. We'd been in trouble before. We'd fallen, broken bones, had the police stop us because we were being little hooligans. "Trouble" for a young mind can mean a lot of things, terrifying things, but rarely did it have any permanence. Of course, that changed a little when Matt died. But it still felt so far away, so removed. Something that could only happen to someone else. Not me.

To our surprise, the door opened. Chrissy smiled. I worried she'd be pissed we bothered her, but nope. She was all smiles. Happy to see us. She said she'd be right out, and within a few minutes, we were all moving off the steps, so she could lay down her speakers.

Jesse asked her what she had been up to, and she said listening to music inside. Billy asked why with an almost accusatory voice, as if her actions directly affected our day. Like she could have known we played football that day, that she was a part of our ritual, and worse, that her absence from it hurt us in ways none of us knew how.

"It felt weird out today," she said, and somehow everyone accepted that. Not me, though. I kept my fear to myself, but when I drank down her words, they didn't sit well in my stomach, turning it like a blender blade. Because she was right. She'd always been smarter than us. It felt weird out today. So why the fuck did we come out?

The radio played a band called Lifetime. I still remember that because out of everything I moved away from after that day, Lifetime was the one thing I took with me. I still listen to their album *Background* once in a while. Jesus. I used to listen to their song "Ghost" on repeat, zoning off into another world, and I never understood why that song had such a profound effect on me until right now. It was the one thread still connecting to that day, the one piece that never split.

As we all sat there joking around, the radio blasting, a thought came over me. Everyone had calmed once Chrissy came out, as if her meeting us on the steps fixed the cracks in our ritual, but it hadn't. She was still inside when we got there. We had to knock. That was different. Regardless of what happened after, those empty steps had existed. We forced it, and that automatically changed the happenstance of our routine. It was supposed to happen naturally, and when it didn't, we should have taken that as a warning. The empty steps told us a secret, and we ignored it. They said to turn around. They said to run away. They said to forget the day ever existed. We didn't listen. We never listened. Maybe we couldn't. Maybe we didn't control the strings. Even then.

How else can I explain why we ignored all the warning signs?

The speakers played a curated playlist made by Chrissy, so it wasn't a radio malfunction when the static came on. I can't believe we continued on with our day after the voices broke through the speakers. The whispers.

INAUDIBLE

CRYING

I'm just remembering the words now, and it's giving me chills as if I'm hearing it for the first time all over again.

"Have you me." That's what it said. Over and over. "Have you me." It spoke in whispers, but the volume coming through the speakers was louder than the music had been. It was so loud, so powerful. "Have you me."

Chrissy's eyes widened, and she ripped the wires off the speakers, but it still whispered. "Have you me."

"I told you it felt weird today," she said, yelling at us as she ran inside, slamming the door behind her. She left the speakers. "Have you me," they said. "Have you me."

Why did we keep walking? Why didn't we turn around? If we had, would the horror have followed us? Did it matter the destination? I don't know.

THE FOLLOWING CONVERSATION HAPPENED IN A SERIES OF EMAILS BETWEEN AUTHOR GAGE GREENWOOD AND CHRISSY HESTER FROM 09/01/24 TO 09/23/24:

GAGE: Thank you so much for agreeing to talk to me, and I completely understand wanting to stick to emails. I guess my first question is, did you get to hear the voice recordings Chris left? Or did you just read about them like I did?

CHRISSY: No problem. Honestly, it feels good to finally be talking about this stuff. All these years, I've been holding on to all of it. The police talked to me after the recordings came out, but it's not the same as getting my story out there. I'm nervous, though. It almost feels like freeing the words and putting them into the atmosphere puts me in danger. If that makes sense. I don't think it does, though. I think I'm separated from them enough. But it's still scary. I'm a teacher now. My priority is the kids I teach. I've tried so hard to keep the past in the past, but it was always with me. If Chris was telling the truth that they all forgot about that day, it may have been a blessing for them. Because I never forgot. Never. There isn't a day where it doesn't creep back into my mind, where I don't feel my heart plummet into my guts.

To answer your question, yes, the police played me the recordings and asked me to verify some of them. Only some of it, though, because they didn't believe most of it worthy of exploring. They didn't care to investigate the unusual, just the lies.

GAGE: I can imagine it was a hard thing to hold onto. So, you mentioned they wanted to know the lies. Were there a lot of lies? Let's start with the music. Did the speakers really turn to static and then to whispers? I suppose you wouldn't know what was true and false after that when they left your house. But what other truths and lies can you tell me about?

CHRISSY: The lies were minor, to be honest. Little things. I didn't think Jesse flirted with me very much, but Chris did. Maybe he downplayed that because he was speaking to his wife? I don't know. The stuff about the voices was all true. Worse, actually, because he didn't know the whole truth on that one either. When I went inside, I stayed on the other side of the door. My heart was pounding in my chest. I could hear them all freaking out on the steps. After a few minutes, the whispers stopped.

Pete and Corey kept saying they wanted to go home. Billy got mad about it. Told them he was going to the bridge with or without them. Jesse kept calling them pussies. Finally, they all agreed to keep going when Chris snapped and yelled at them to stop arguing, saying they were following Billy wherever he wanted to go. That was another lie he told in his recordings, pretending he was just going along with it all.

As soon as they left down the road, I popped the door open and brought the speakers in. When I placed them on the coffee table in the living room, the voices came back. I have no witnesses to prove that, but it's true.

GAGE: What did they say???? Was it the same thing? Have you me?

CHRISSY: No. They said, "Stay." Over and over and over again. "Stay." After a minute or two, they said it so much and so fast it blended together and just sounded like hissing. SSSSSSSSSSSSSSSSSSSSSSSSSSSSSSS. But if I listened closely, I could hear the "tay" part too.

GAGE: Jeez. That must have been terrifying. What did you do?

CHRISSY: You said I wouldn't know what happened after they left, but you'd be wrong. Because I did the thing I had wanted to do since the first time those idiots stopped by. I followed them. Maybe I wanted to say "fuck you" to the voices. Maybe I had my own strings pulling me along. Probably, though, I was just scared to be alone with weird fucking voices coming through my speakers. But I always wanted to know what those boys got into, and I found out. Oh, I found out. Unfortunately, I found a lot more, too.

THE FOLLOWING TRANSCRIPT COMES FROM A VOICE RECORDER APP ON CHRIS MCDONALD'S IPHONE, DATED 08/08/23. THIS FOURTH RECORDING STARTED AT 7:15 PM:

Sorry for the abrupt ending to the last recording. I got a little freaked out. I almost turned around and came home. Anyway, Chrissy freaked out and went inside and the rest of us argued about what we should do next. Billy really wanted to keep going, but I kept insisting we should turn around. The whole day was fucking me up. It was all just off. The rest of the guys started piling on me, so I relented. Against my better judgment.

I'm at the bridge now for the next part of our story. I just drove away from Chrissy's old house. What a fucking creeper I am, sitting in front of a house, staring at it, while talking into my phone.

LAUGHTING

I wonder if Chrissy still lives there. How would I know?

SIGHING

Anyway, as I said, I'm at the bridge now. Well, I'm not, because the bridge isn't there anymore. It got torn down a few years ago, I think. I'm next to where the bridge was. On the end of a dead-end street.

It hadn't been used in forever, even when we were kids. It was just a rusty old bridge that cars couldn't drive on. We had to walk through ten feet of shrubs to get on it. There were two huge billboards facing traffic, and their backs were facing us on the bridge. Perfect white rectangles the size of small houses, prime for us to graffiti. And who would give a shit? No one saw the backs of them unless they were other idiots walking over a defunct bridge that led only to more shrubs and the train tracks.

It was weird hanging out with those guys. We could be freaked out, and the next minute, we were back to fucking around and forgetting everything. On the bridge, we were quiet at first. Pete had a backpack with him, and he dropped it on the cement. He pulled out some cans of spray paint and we took turns grabbing a can and doodling on the sign. Within minutes, we were all laughing and goofing with one another. Matt, the noise, the whispers. That all went away. And I don't think it was the thing in our brains this time. I think it was just living. Being kids. We didn't need an outside force to make us forget. We had the power of friendship.

Billy spray-painted Matt's name with the day he died under it. After that, we all came over and put our initials under it. I guess that was our way of saying goodbye. Corey sat down with his legs crossed and ate some candy he had in his pockets. He told us he didn't know what he'd do without us, that he felt so weak, and for the first time, none of us had a smartass joke to make, because we all felt the same way. Cars were rushing under us. Giant billboards blocked the last remnants of sun, towering over us like square ghosts. On the opposite side, giant letters told drivers passing by what they should buy at the store. We were so fucking small. Sometimes it's hard to picture how small you are, but when those moments come, when something reminds you, it's crippling.

Any one of those cars zipping by below us could end up on a road we'd walk down, spiraling out of control and taking us out of the world. Our legacy too short to matter. We'd be forgotten quicker than the graffiti we sprayed all over the blank white spaces.

Jesse came and put his arm around Corey. We all just sat

there for a while, creating a circle around Corey. Billy told us his mother hadn't slept since Matt died, and he worried she'd go next, a victim to her own grief. Funny enough, she outlived most of us in that circle. As far as I know, she's still kicking.

Pete barely said a word. He rarely did. He was a shy kid, but once in a while, he'd break out of his shell and really get talkative and start coming up with all these weird, creative ideas for us. I remember one time, he talked all of us into shoveling snow at the end of our driveways, and then we dug into them to build a sort of igloo nook. Then we all took walkie-talkies and chatted with each other. But he set all the channels before giving them to us, only one of us would have the talkie with the wrong channel on it. So, when we spoke to each other, we'd all figure out who was on the line, and the person left out would be the one we'd attack with snowballs while he waited in his igloo. It was stupid and fun and creative.

Somewhere in our timelines, we lost that. We still had fun. We still acted stupid. And sometimes we were even creative. But almost never were we all three. I think that's the tragedy of growing up. Those strings get separated.

But Pete, well, he still knew how to pull them together once in a while.

He had a sharpie on him, and he said we should play a game where he drew a picture on the back of the billboard but covered it up with his shirt. Then, the next person in line would get a quick peak at it, and he'd have to draw it next, covering his drawing so no one else could see. Next person does the same thing, until the five of us all drew the picture, and we would see what it looked like at the end. Basically, a picture version of the game telephone.

It wasn't very original. There was a handheld video game that did the same thing. Can't remember the name of it now. Can't even remember the system it was on, but I remember playing the game at Pete's house once. But it felt original at the time. I think we were all looking for something to anchor us to the bridge.

So, Pete took his shirt off, grabbed the marker, and doodled on the billboard. He had this weird thing where he always stuck his tongue out when he got into something, letting it dangle out the side of his mouth. He covered his work with his hand until he finished, and then he draped his shirt over it.

I went next. He pulled the shirt away, just a little, and I cracked up. He drew Jesse with a giant ass and a gas cloud surrounding him like he'd just let out a mega fart. Jesse had a scar going from his cheek to his left eye from when his cousin slit his face with a knife when they were nine. His cousin was a fucking nut job. I don't remember what caused the fight between them, but does it matter? What possesses a nine-year-old to swing a knife at his cousin? Jesse's attitude grew after that. The scar turning into a chip on his shoulder. Anyway, the line going from mouth to eye in Pete's drawing made it clear who the sketch was meant to be. Pete knew Jesse could kick his ass, but he also knew Jesse wouldn't. He had to get his digs where he could, because Jesse had a much better chance at dating Chrissy than he did.

I copied the picture the best I could, and one by one, the rest of them took their turns until Billy went last. If I had known where the game was gonna go, I would have paid better attention to when the laughing stopped.

Pete revealed his picture first, and we all craned our heads to get a good look at it. Remember, we were all covering our pictures with our shirts too, so we couldn't all gather around the picture. Everyone giggled. Even Jesse, although he added a, "Go fuck yourself," to the end of it.

I revealed my picture, and it was a fairly good replica of Pete's, but I didn't add the scar. Didn't feel a second stab at the kid's weak spot was needed.

Corey went next. To be fair to him, I only gave him the

quickest glance. He had the fart cloud, and the giant ass, but no person attached to the ass. It was like two circles merging into each other, surrounded by a puffy cloud.

"I didn't see Jesse in the fart!" Corey said, red-faced and wheezing from laughing.

Jesse shook his head with a smile crawling up one cheek as he pulled his shirt away from his picture. He had the cloud, and the giant ass, but he must have confused what the ass was. He drew two big black circles within each bigger circle, so the ass now looked like two goofy eyes.

Billy chuckled and pulled his shirt off. It was basically the same as Jesse's, but the eyes were a little less circular, sharper.

We laughed at each other for a while. Talked some shit. And moved on. That was it. No weird noises, no radio whispers. Maybe if something weird happened, we wouldn't have gone to the last stop. Maybe we would have finally convinced ourselves it was too much. But we missed the warning. We completely missed it.

INAUDIBLE

LOUD BREATHING

Julia, it's all starting to get really clear in my head. I remember so much now. I don't think I should be doing this. It was a mistake to remember. But it's too late now. I have to finish this.

SOUNDS OF A CAR STARTING

BEEPING

The warning we received on the bridge was Billy's picture.

I'll start a new recording on the train tracks.

THE FOLLOWING ENTRY COMES FROM WILLIAM HUFFMAN'S DIARY, THE SECOND ENTRY IN HIS JOURNAL DATED 09/05/2009:

It's late now. My parents are asleep. I can't stop thinking about how phony everyone was at the wake. Is this what we are all destined for? Everyone forgetting to love you when you're here, only to pretend they did when you're gone?

One time, Matt and I were hanging out in the woods behind our house, and we just started digging a hole, trying to see how big we could make it in the few hours we had. I don't remember who started the digging, or why the other joined in. There really wasn't any communication. Someone dug, and the other joined in. No purpose, no reasoning. We just dug and kept digging until it was time to stop.

That's kind of how I feel all the time.

Always digging a hole for no reason.

I heard something weird out the window a little while ago, like a whisper. For about ten minutes, I convinced myself it was Matt trying to talk to me, but eventually I realized it was just a branch scraping on the side of the house that I'd tricked myself was a voice.

Still, though, it really sounded like, "Know when to stop."

But what would that even mean?

Know when to stop.

I'm thirteen and I don't think I've ever even started anything. I feel like nothing. Empty. Hollow. Useless.

Know when to stop? Someone tell me where to start.

THE FOLLOWING TRANSCRIPT COMES FROM A VOICE RECORDER APP ON CHRIS MCDONALD'S IPHONE, DATED 08/08/23. THIS FIFTH RECORDING STARTED AT 8:09 PM:

Oh God, Julia, this is all wrong. I feel awful. Not sick, just fucked up. You know the feeling you get in a house when the wiring is messed up? That's how I feel. I shouldn't have come here. I know that now. I knew it then, all those years ago, but something pulled us, and it's pulling me now.

The train doesn't run through here anymore, but the tracks are still there, rusted thick slabs of metal. The homeless hut is there, though, and that's why we all came here during our rituals.

It's a sizable fort, built from huge chunks of picket fences, all tossed around each other into a crooked, haphazard square. Inside the fort, there was a small mound of wood, charred and blackened. We knew homeless folks stayed there, but we never saw them. We'd have assumed they'd abandoned it if not for the occasional food wrapper or nip bottle.

It was out in the open, tucked near the outline of oaks traveling along the tracks about fifteen feet from where trains would blast by. But even tucked, it was very easy to spot. No one seemed to care. No one tore it down.

When we hung out there, it was just to be loud and stupid. We didn't cause trouble, or drink, or anything like that. We had some kind of unspoken thing about wanting to show respect for the place, not wanting to ruin it for whoever needed it to live. I don't remember ever being scared a homeless person would show up and flip out on us. What if the people living there were dangerous?

The hut isn't there anymore. I'm staring at the spot it used to be, and there isn't any hint of it, no ghosts. It's just me in my car. Nothing else around. They don't even have any lights coming through from the streets above. It's fucking cold and dark here, a little hidden nightmare in the middle of a town full of bad dreams.

There's still a blank spot in my memory. For a long time, it was filled in with fiction, but now it's wide open. The problem is the truth hasn't replaced it yet, so it's like a dank hole in my skull. But I feel something trying to fill it in and it's terrifying me.

I guess I should start with what I do remember. We were all sitting in the hut, and it was fine and good. I don't remember the conversations, but they were just the normal bullshit kid talk stuff. Probably girls, sports, music, bullshit.

But it got heavy. Corey got all watery-eyed and told us he

didn't know if he was going to stay in Rhode Island anymore. His mother and stepfather were assholes, and he'd been cracking away at the idea of moving in with his real father in Massachusetts. A single state away. No more than an hour and a half. We'd still see him from time to time. His dad would pick us up and bring us to hang out on weekends or something. But we all knew once he left, we'd visit once or twice, and eventually, the space between us would fill in with new friends, new lives.

We were losing another one of the ritual friends, and that meant we were losing the ritual. We all must have known the ritual was dying that night before Corey said what he said, but his speech dropped the final nail in. This was it.

Jesse said, "Then we need to make tonight matter."

Pete flicked a pebble at him and said, "What do you have in mind?"

Jesse shrugged. We had no idea how to make the night count. Special times weren't made, they just invaded your space when you least expected it.

INAUDIBLE

LOUD BREATHING

Oh my God.

CAR STARTING

I remember now. I need to get the fuck out of here.

CAR TURNING OFF

BANGING

Fuck. Fuck. Fuck.

LOUD STATIC

MUSIC BLASTING

CAR DOOR OPENING

SOUNDS OF FOOTSTEPS RUNNING ON LOOSE STONES

Julia. Oh my God. I need you to listen to me. It's real. All of it is real. Holy fuck. Are they here now? Are they still here?

HEAVY BREATHING

They came out of the woods. We were leaving the hut to check out the train coming in because we heard the tracks rumble, and they were there. They came out of the woods.

A ROUGH INDISTINGUISHABLE SOUND

Fuck. I have to get out of here. The car won't start. I'm running. Julia, if something happens to me, I love you.

HEAVY BREATHING

THE FOLLOWING TRANSCRIPT COMES FROM A VOICEMAIL LEFT ON JULIA MCDONALD'S IPHONE BY CHRIS MCDONALD:

Julia. I had to call you. You're probably on the other line trying to find me. I left you a bunch of recordings on my phone. They're in the voice recorder app. My password is G-R-4-E-L-F-@-@. All caps. Listen to the recordings. I'm hiding in the woods. I don't know if I'm coming home. I don't know if I'm ever going to make it home, but I'm going to try. I love you so much.

THE FOLLOWING IS A TRANSCRIPT FROM AN INTERVIEW WITH JESSE CAPALDI WITH THE WARWICK POLICE DEPARTMENT ON 09/03/23:

OFFICER DUCHANE: What about the whispers on the radio? Did you hear those too?

JESSE CAPALDI: Yes.

OFFICER FAZZIO: So, it's safe to say weird shit was happening to you all day?

JESSE CAPALDI: I guess so.

OFFICER DUCHANE: So, what happened at the train tracks?

SILENCE

OFFICER FAZZIO: Jesse? What happened at the train tracks?

JESSE CAPALDI: I'll tell you what Chris said to me the night he called now.

SILENCE

OFFICER DUCHANE: Okay. Let's hear it.

JESSE CAPALDI: He was winded, like he'd been running for a while. He said he called his wife right before he called me and left her a voice message because he didn't think he would live through the night.

I thought he was talking about suicide, so I got really nervous. I asked him to calm down and tell me what was going on. Keep in mind, a few of our friends from that night ended up killing themselves.

OFFICER DUCHANE: Pete Peratta, and Corey George. In fact, you and Chris are the only two still alive, no?

JESSE CAPALDI: (Laughing.) Do you really think he's still alive?

OFFICER FAZZIO: We hope so. That's one of the many things we're trying to figure out here. So, you were telling us about the phone call.

JESSE CAPALDI: I was worried he was going to kill himself. He sounded… Bad. In trouble. Hurting. You know? But then he told me he was in the woods by the tracks, and that just sent a chill up my spine. He asked if I remembered what happened that night, meaning the night with Billy. I said I did, and at the time, I thought I had remembered, but I was wrong.

SILENCE

OFFICER FAZZIO: What do you mean you were wrong?

JESSE CAPALDI: He kept drilling into me. "Do you remember? Do you really remember?" And it was like each time he asked, I felt my brain cracking, and this layer of hard clay crumbled to the floor, freeing my mind. Everything I thought I knew about my life. It was all a lie. He asked me if I ever felt weird seeing him when we ran into each other after that day, and I did. Like this weird static pull, an electric shock traveling up my skin.

He asked if I remembered the sound in the field, and until

he asked, I hadn't. He asked if I remembered the whispers on the radio, and until he asked, I hadn't. He asked if I remembered Billy's picture on the billboard, and until he asked, I hadn't.

SILENCE

SNIFFLING

And he asked if I remembered the men with the white faces and black pools for eyes coming out of the woods.

SILENCE

And until he asked.

SILENCE

I hadn't.

THE FOLLOWING CONVERSATION HAPPENED IN A SERIES OF EMAILS BETWEEN AUTHOR GAGE GREENWOOD AND CHRISSY HESTER ROM 09/01/24 TO 09/23/24:

GAGE: Okay, so moving on to the bridge. Since I now know you followed them. Was that all true? The picture Billy drew? Did it really look like how he described?

CHRISSY: Okay, so this was the biggest lie he told, but it was so innocuous, I have to presume he either didn't remember correctly or just clouded his memory because of what happened after. Oh, there's also another big lie. The biggest, but I'll save that until we get there. For now, here's the truth of the bridge:

The picture did look weird. Calling it eyes in a cloud is a bit far-fetched, but I guess I can see it. To me, they looked more like crescent moons. But here's the thing. Billy didn't draw that. Billy went first after Pete. Chris went last. HE drew the weird picture. I don't know why he changed that.

The rest of his story on the bridge is true.

GAGE: Okay, what about the train tracks? The hut, all of that, real? And obviously, I'm building toward the things in the woods. I had no idea you followed them when we started this interview. You may be the only witness left to all of this. Were there really things in the woods?

CHRISSY: The hut was there. Everyone knew about that place, but most kids didn't go down there. Jesus, who knew what kind of weirdos hung out there. Homeless or not, it was clear someone lived there, and would you go trouncing into any stranger's house? I know I wouldn't.

So, to the big question. Yes, his story is true… But with a caveat…

THE FOLLOWING TRANSCRIPT COMES FROM A VOICE RECORDER APP ON CHRIS MCDONALD'S IPHONE, DATED 08/08/23. THIS SIXTH RECORDING STARTED AT 8:17 PM:

I called you and left a message. I called Jesse. He knows now. He remembers too. I'm not crazy. I think they're here.

GASPING

They came out of the woods from a white mist. Three of them. They had pale skin and black, sunken eyes. No mouths. No noses. At the same time they came out, the train came by, screaming. Those trains are so loud, it's deafening. But even with that, we could HEAR the things talking to us. They spoke in these screechy voices, and their words went right into our brains. It hurt to hear them. It hurt.

"Have you us," they said. Over and over. "Have you us."

We all pushed off each other, stepping back, getting ready to run, but at the same time, it was like we couldn't run. Oh my God. I can't unsee their faces now. It's horrible. Jesus. They were terrifying.

CRYING

Jesus, Julia, they're here. I can feel them.

We kept yelling, "RUN! RUN!" to each other, but Billy kept stepping forward.

Jesus. Oh fuck. They're here.

INAUDIBLE

Julia, help me.
LOUD RINGING
Billy wouldn't run. We reached out for him and tried to pull him back, but he stepped forward.
DISTORTED SCREECHING
Come on Billy. Billy, don't go.
LOUD SCREECHING
They took him and we fell over screaming. It was like they squeezed our brains. It hurt deep in our skulls.
*DISTORTED SCREECHING *
And then we stood up and went home. Like nothing happened.
Corey killed himself a little while later.
Pete, a year or two after that.
Fuck.
They are here. I can hear them moving in the brush.
All that's left is me and Jesse.
I don't know what happened to Billy. I don't know what they did to him.
LOUD SCREECHING
CHRIS SCREAMING
They're here. I can see them. Oh. Fuck. I can see them. They're real. Help me!
SCREECHING
DISTORTED VIBRATING
Help me!
SCREAMING
Help!
WHOOSHING
HELP!
CHRIS SCREAMING
Please! Fuck! No! Don't!
DON'T!
PLEASE!
SCREAMING

DISTORTED SCREECHING
No.
No!
Please.
Stop.
Stop!
SILENCE
CLICKING
MUFFLED BREATHING
CLICKING
SILENCE
LOUD SCREECHING

THE FOLLOWING IS A TRANSCRIPT FROM AN INTERVIEW WITH JESSE CAPALDI WITH THE WARWICK POLICE DEPARTMENT ON 09/03/23:

JESSE CAPALDI: They're in my head! GET THEM OUT. GET THEM OUT!

SHOUTING

OFFICER FAZZIO: Sit down! Sit down!

OFFICER DUCHANE: Hey! Sit down.

SHOUTING

ROUGH BANGING

A GUNSHOT

THE FOLLOWING CONVERSATION HAPPENED IN A SERIES OF EMAILS BETWEEN AUTHOR GAGE GREENWOOD AND CHRISSY HESTER FROM 09/01/24 TO 09/23/24:

GAGE: So, your full story is that some things came out of the woods and took Billy? I just want to make sure I understand it correctly.

CHRISSY: Yes. Chris was telling the truth.

GAGE: So, when the narrative came out that Billy ran into the woods on his own and disappeared, why didn't you come forward, since you said you remembered it all, even if they forgot?

CHRISSY: Come on! Are you really asking why a 15-year-old girl didn't come forward to say strange alien men came from the woods and stole a boy, despite four other witnesses saying something different? Do you not think maybe I questioned my own sanity, my own experiences, my own eyes and ears? With the exception of how horrible I feel for Chris and his wife and Jesse and his family, it was a relief when this all came out, to know I wasn't alone. I wasn't crazy. We all saw it. We all saw what happened.

GAGE: Fair enough. Do you worry about what happened to all of them? That it will happen to you too?

CHRISSY: Of course! I have severe anxiety to begin with. But I think they never got in my brain like they did the rest. I've never forgotten what I saw. I was far enough away. The aliens or whatever they were didn't see me, didn't know I was there. That's my best guess as to why my experiences have been so different after that day.

GAGE: That brings me to the caveat you mentioned, which I presume is the big lie? You said Chris had one big lie, is that the caveat you were speaking about?

CHRISSY: Yes. In the recordings, he talked about all of them trying to run, but how they were kind of stuck, and they reached for Billy, trying to stop him from moving forward. That was lie.

GAGE: It's kind of understandable, though. Scared kids. They probably wouldn't consider each other, wouldn't look out for each other. They'd just want to run.

CHRISSY: You misunderstood me. I should have just said it in my last email, but honestly, typing it kind of freaked me out. I was thinking maybe I could avoid it, but I'm doing this to tell the truth, so I need to tell the whole truth.

They weren't trying to run. The way Billy stepped forward? They all did. They all pushed each other out of the way and walked forward. Once they realized they were competition with each other, like they were playing Red Light, Green Light, they yelled to the things. "Take me. Take me. Not him. Me."

They fought over who would go. Billy turned to them, tears pouring down his face, and said, "It has to me. You took me out today to help me, so help me. Let this be my turn."

And they all listened. They backed off. But yeah, they weren't trying to run away. They had wanted to go with those fucking things. I know it sounds crazy, and trust me, their reaction to the things is a huge reason I doubted myself. Like, maybe it what I saw wasn't aliens. Maybe it was people in costumes. Maybe it was the homeless people that lived in the huts. Maybe they knew these people, talked to them before, and this was all planned. Maybe these were predators who convinced these poor fucking kids that they were going to take one of them somewhere special, but when Billy didn't come back, they covered their asses and made up a story about Billy running away. But that never explained how the things from the woods said nearly the same sentence I heard whispered on the radio. And, of course, any concern I had on that front ended when I heard the recordings, and about Chris's phone.

THE FOLLOWING CONVERSATION HAPPENED IN A SERIES OF EMAILS BETWEEN AUTHOR GAGE GREENWOOD AND OFFICER LEJUENE FROM 09/20/24 TO 09/21/24:

GAGE: Thanks so much for agreeing to talk to me. I guess my first question is what made the phone so special? I mean, I'm assuming a lot of folks lose their phones, and different places have lost and founds, but how did the phone end up in the possession of the police department in the first place, and once you had it, what made you search the phone to find the audio recordings?

OFFICER LEJUENE: We were called about the phone by

a couple of hikers who found it in the woods. And you're right, they probably wouldn't have called us over a random cell phone in the woods, unless they suspected something had happened to the owner of the phone, which they didn't in this case. They called us to tell us it was glowing.

Our dispatcher said, "Glowing? What the fuck do you mean?" Not in those words, but you catch my drift. They said it was emanating light, a glowing green color. And because they'd watched too many *The Simpsons* episodes, they equated a green glow with something nuclear. So, my partner and I went down to check it out, and the phone was not glowing. They swore it had been, and that the glowing slowly diminished before we got there.

I threw on some gloves and tossed the phone in our car, which, in hindsight, was stupid. I had just assumed the hikers were high off their minds or something, but I should have been more careful, just in case it did have some weird radiation or something.

Anyway, we drove back to the station thinking nothing of it. We have protocol for lost and found items, and it wasn't really my concern what the fuck happened to the phone after I brought it in, but then it rang. Gal's number came up. Julia, who we all know now was Chris's wife.

My partner and I look at each other, and debate on answering it. You're not supposed to, believe it or not, but I said fuck it. We could find out who it belonged to in seconds.

As soon as I picked up, she was in a panic. "CHRIS! CHRIS! What's going on?"

I explained who I was, and she said she got a voicemail from Chris freaking out, saying he was in the woods and that he had recorded some messages for her on a voice recorder app. Now, I started to get a little perked up because the phone was found in the woods. It didn't feel like an accidental drop anymore. Maybe something happened to Chris. So, I started prying on what she knew about his whereabouts, what his plans were, blah blah. Meanwhile, my partner is getting ready to call into the station for a missing persons.

She said he was supposed to be home hours ago from work, and I asked where she lived. I didn't recognize the street name, so I asked what town she was in, and she says, "Westerly." I'm like, "Westerly? Where the fuck is that?" and she sounds surprised when she says, "Rhode Island?"

I laughed, which I know is terrible, but it shocked me. I said, "Well, he certainly wasn't going to be home on time. His phone was found in Fox Glen Park in Mansfield, Ohio."

She was irate. Said I must have that wrong. She's checking to make sure she called the right number. She's totally insane about this. Said there's no way. He went to work that morning in Providence.

As you can guess, this caused a lot of confusion. She told us to check the voice recordings, absolutely insistent on it. She even gave us his phone's password, but we never needed it. Would we have been able to answer his phone if it was locked? Anyway, as you can guess, the recordings didn't help us with our confusion, and to be quite frank, they spooked me the fuck out. If you've only read the transcripts, I assure you they don't do justice to how weird some of those sounds were at the end.

Obviously, once the story broke, and everything was crazy, we did all the things. Tracking where the phone was when he made his last calls. Sure enough, Cranston, Rhode Island. I mean, how the fuck does that happen? We've tried every explanation in the book to figure out how someone makes phone calls while in Cranston, Rhode Island, and one hour later, his phone is found in Mansfield, Ohio. It doesn't make sense. Every explanation we've thought of or come across has a million holes. Chris went to work that day and left around five o'clock. His phone was found at 9:30 in Fox Glen Park. Unless he flew, he couldn't get from point A to point B in that time. And those recordings don't indicate any travel. Nothing about it adds up.

GAGE: So, what's your leading guess as to what happened to Chris?

OFFICER LEJUENE: Honestly, little fucking green men.

THE FOLLOWING ENTRY COMES FROM WILLIAM HUFFMAN'S DIARY, DATED 09/07/2009.

I am not me anymore.

* * *

I've always loved a good alien story, and I have wanted to write one for a long time. Recently, I had that opportunity, when I was asked to write a novella for one of the Dark Tides books by Crystal Lake Publishing. In that book, I will share the pages with John Durgin and Andrew Van Wey, something I'm thrilled about. When I was conceptualizing the story I wanted to write for Dark Tides, my concepts split off into two directions. One is the story I submitted to Dark Tides, a closed-in alien story, where we only see a few people affected, as opposed to an alien invasion story that affects the entire world. It involves a sister and brother, and their relationship through the years while an alien slowly destroys one of them from the inside. The other story I came up with is the one you just read. I loved the idea of the mystery unfolding through various transcripts, and from that, I really wanted to tell a story of dissolving friendships. There's sadness in memories, even the good ones. I do not wish to be young again. I'm happy with the life I have now, but I miss those friends I hung out with, believing we could take over the world together, unafraid of anything, while secretly afraid of everything. This story has a self-insert, which I did because it's my story. It is me re-examining my old friendships (the names have been changed to protect the innocent), going through things I actually did in my life, and turning them into terror.

A SERIES OF ATTACKS

Brian clenched his jaw and scrunched his brow, creating a show for the two detectives haunting the corners of his hospital room. The one with the mustache—circa 1970—stood with his arms crossed, mimicking Brian's facial movements, feigning sympathy. The other, a young redheaded woman, chewed on the inside of her cheek, letting her impatience out on the wall with dancing fingertips.

"Try to think about the sounds and smells. Sometimes that helps people remember," the woman said.

Brian didn't need help remembering. He certainly didn't need some oblique sensory method to pierce into his mind. After all, there was something completely un-Freudian about homemade bombs. The details of his experience were clear, but he didn't see the boy, or even the explosion until the dust and wind had begun to topple him. All of his focus had been on the woman, leaving him with very little to offer the detectives. Still, he should play along, and let them dissect his memory.

The ghosts crowded him, both when he had his eyes opened and when he had them closed. The ones that materialized in recall were sure to be dead, or at the very least, fractions of who they once were. The two that lingered like creeping ivy in this room, flanking in the corners so that when one was in focus, the other fogged in his peripherals, might as well have been spirits, apparitions struggling to matter. They were epitaphs: the final words on what has already been written.

He brought himself back to the bus stop, looking forward upon a manifold of thirty or so people. The bitter morning air gave signs of relenting to the afternoon sun. Most of the snow had melted into slush and browned from the accosting exhaust of nearby traffic. It slurped around his feet, suctioning and seeping into the soles of his shoes, drenching his socks. It penetrated and made the cardboard hospital bed sheets feel like ice against his toes. He had to remind himself to stay in the past, to be at the bus stop.

The 8 to Walton took an obtrusive turn onto the bend and its metal bones let out a series of violent belches as it bobbled along a minefield of potholes. The brakes screeched and hissed, and the crowd of people dissipated into two smaller groups: those that would definitely die that day, and those that had a slight chance of living. From that morning forward, Brian's life was a reward for only one reason, because his bus was not the one headed to Walton.

Then he thought about the Hispanic lady—the tall, lithe woman who always wore the flounce skirts and, morning after morning, shot flirtatious eyes across the crowd: a jolt of early-day adrenaline for Brian. He tried to focus on her, forcing his mind to adjust and see things it probably had not seen to begin with. Which group took her in their current? As far as he could piece together, she didn't ride either wave. Instead, she seemed to float into a third space made up of just her and an ethereal glow, looking beyond the people, smiling toward Brian. His eyes began to water as he recognized the absence of truth in the ridiculously magical vision. The gray and dirty cloud must have swallowed her the way it ate the lives of so many that morning.

"What are you remembering, son?" The man said.

"It's all just shapes. No details," he lied, not wanting to talk any longer.

The pretty redhead sighed. "Anything could be helpful."

"The boy killed himself too. He was on the bus. It's not like he could do it again. Why do you need any more information than that?"

The man uncrossed his arms and leaned forward. "We're just trying to make sense of it all. Fill in all the pieces."

Brian knew he was lying. He had read today's paper, which said the police were worried this was the first in a series of attacks and that the boy may have been working with others who wanted to create mass hysteria. Who would really be more culpable for mass hysteria, a potentially nonexistent group of teens, or the police who announced them into reality? More importantly, why wouldn't these officers tell him what the newspapers already knew and reported?

He used his forearms to scoot himself into an upright position, wincing as a burst of pain blasted from his ribs to his brain. His arms trembled and his breath caught in his lungs. The redhead pushed herself out of the corner, moving toward him slowly enough to make it obvious there was no genuine interest in helping him out. He lifted his shaking hand to let her know he was all set.

"Look, I don't think I can help you out right now. I need to be alone."

The detectives looked at each other, employing no effort to hide their disappointment. The man with the mustache darted his eyes from the woman to the door. She seemed to understand.

"Okay, well if you think of anything, will you please give us a call?" As she said this, she placed her card on his bedside tray table and flicked the corner of it in a deliberate and pushy motion. He nodded.

As they headed for the door, an excitement expanded inside of him and his muscles tensed. He closed his eyes, heading toward the Hispanic girl, her flounce skirts, and the way she bit her bottom lip when she looked at him. His breath quickened as the detectives disappeared, and the slush pooled around his feet. He tunneled toward the past.

The door to his hospital room caught in mid-close and sprung open. His wife crossed the threshold.

After weeks in a hospital bed, Brian returned home. His wife hooked her arm around his and walked him inside, treating him like an old man, crooked and broken. There was no fanfare, no committee of family and friends flocking inside waiting to express their gratitude to the lord almighty that he survived such a tragic event. The entire first day went by as uneventfully as could possibly be, and for that Brian was grateful, not to the lord almighty, but to Charlotte for knowing him well enough to call off the horde days in advance, suggesting they give him time to heal before overwhelming him with their presence.

He spent most of the day on the couch watching television, drinking beers against doctor's orders, and letting the alcohol and pain meds create a delightful fog. His wife made him sandwiches and handed them to him with self-congratulatory smirks as if deli meat and seven-grain bread would redress the damage caused by the boy and his bomb. Mostly, his day slithered away into nothingness, just as it had before the bombing. Traumatic events cause people to make drastic changes in their lives, except when they don't.

That night, while Charlotte plucked away at her teeth in what was her normal nightly tooth care ritual, Brian decided to stave off sleep for a half hour or so and slunk downstairs into the kitchen for a snack and another beer. As he poured the beer into a mug, the headline on the Tanner's Switch Press, sticking out amongst a stack of unopened mail as if it were crawling out of the pile—read me, please!—caught his eye. The Walton Victims: Who They Were. Forgetting the snack, Brian sat down with his beer and pulled the paper toward him.

The front page told the reader how it was important not to focus on the tragic side of the bombing, but instead, to celebrate the lives of those who were lost that day. Brian skimmed past this and unfurled the paper to the guts of the article. As it opened, the pages wavered and folded in on themselves, and he knew before he could even see it that his wife had clipped the coupons out. The article was now a series of potholes.

He went over to the junk drawer next to the sink and pulled out Charlotte's accordion coupon purse. There were hundreds of coupons from magazines and newspapers, and some printed from the internet. It would take hours trying to glean the paper back to a whole. He slammed the drawer and went to the refrigerator for another beer.

"Is everything alright?" Charlotte yelled down the stairs.

"It's fine," he yelled back, "but I'm going to sleep down here tonight."

There was no response, not an objection, or an understanding agreement, just silence, followed by the slow tiny tapping of footsteps from the landing back to the bedroom.

Brian grabbed his laptop and sat on the couch. He went to the Tanner's Switch Newspaper's website, hoping to find a replica of the article online, but it wasn't there. Instead, there seemed to be a plethora of articles exploiting the bombing, much like what the front of the print edition claimed the reader shouldn't focus on.

He continued to search the internet for articles about the deceased and found nothing on the victims. However, he did find out that the boy's journals were uncovered. The police were able to conclude that the bombing was the act of one angry individual. They released this information, along with a full printout of the boy's journals, in hopes of alleviating fears. Bring the fear; calm the fear. All in a day's work.

There was something grim and ignoble about the journals being online for anyone to see, but this didn't stop Brian from reading them. The least he could do was try to understand why the boy did what he did. That was probably all the kid wanted anyway.

The night slipped away as he read the journals, the articles, the editorials, the user comments. He read it all, letting each opinion assault him anew. Everyone had a reason for why this happened, they all had a solution, and all of it was nonsense. More God in schools. More money for education. Open carry laws. Parents blamed the school systems and teachers blamed parents.

Brian decided this is why social media is so popular. It creates the illusion that people care what we have to say. It gives us a factitious audience for our opinions when we most desperately need them to be heard. Who can scream the loudest: A new America.

The zeitgeist of our beginnings became a poltergeist in the present. The ideals that once mattered haunt us. The celebration of the individual, the concept of hard work reaping success, the idea that our uniqueness is valuable, all of these beliefs lay phantom in an overpopulated world. One day we woke up, got sucked into the current, shot out in the spume, and distributed amongst a million grains of sand. The spirit of our individual nature drowned and the bridling of our thoughts and ideas suffocated us.

Now, we are desperate to have a voice, so we protest, form political arguments, demand more God, pray for the strengthening of morality, or we build bombs and make our opinions heard in an explosion of dust and metal. It's all just different methods of saying, "Someone, listen to me. Someone care." The truth is, no God, guns, or education could ever repair the overwhelming desire to matter.

In the morning, Brian snuck past the clanging pans and the smell of waffles, limping out the door and toward the gas station at the end of the street. He convinced the bored cashier to check the back room for an extra copy of yesterday's paper, and he paid full price for old news. When he returned home, there was a plate of waffles waiting for him on the coffee table. A folded napkin, a bottle of syrup, and a fork accompanied it.

He sat down and unfolded the paper and the completeness of it sent an eager shiver up his spine. Behind him, his wife's footsteps crept out of the kitchen and moved up the stairs. "You should eat those while they're warm," she said as she ascended.

The article gave the names of each person killed in the bombing and a few sentences describing what they did or who they were. They came from all lifestyles, bringing to this world a variety of gifts, but all of them flowered into nothing more than a blurb outside of the obituaries. It was more than most people got, he supposed.

He thought about the Hispanic girl. There were no pictures to accompany the blurbs, so he had no way of knowing if she was one of the ones listed. He tried to picture her in the descriptions, but they were so vague, she could have fit a number of them. He began to cross out ones that definitely didn't fit. He crossed out the men first, although a few names were ambiguous, and their descriptions didn't let on one way or the other.

Once he eliminated the obvious men, he moved on to other conflicting traits. He scribbled over the grandmother and the 1970s gold medalist. Since he assumed the Hispanic girl was going to work every morning, he doubted that her flounce skirts were mechanic attire. There were still plenty of names left. She could have been the hospice nurse or the engineering student. She could have been the mother of two. She could be more than a few chalky black sentences. She could be alive.

He wrote down the names of every person who could potentially be the Hispanic girl and checked them on all of the social media sites. This proved more difficult than he expected. Some of the names were too common and the profile pictures did little to jog his memory of the people he saw that day at the bus stop. Some of the names drew zero results. This surprised Brian, since most of the people he remembered seeing that day were young. He expected most people under forty to have some sort of social media profile. Maybe some people were satisfied with being unheard.

Facebook did assist him in removing a few names from the list, but it wasn't enough to satisfy him. His interest in finding out what happened to the Hispanic girl began to brew into something bigger. He no longer had a curiosity, but instead, a craving.

A volatile stench of bleach swathed the air. Charlotte must have been cleaning the upstairs bathroom again. If there were an undiscovered, purer form of white, Charlotte would be the one to expose it. When she began cleaning, she vanished into the chore until it was complete. Brian wouldn't exist to her until she purified every inch of the house. He would have the day to himself, undisturbed and free to explore his new riddle further.

The puzzle would expand, though, and soon Brian would find himself swallowed deep into an obsession. He would spend the next few weeks digging into every crevice of the bombing story, looking to find the one soul who seemed to vaporize within the cloud that haunted the bus stop, as if she hadn't lived or died that day, but instead, never existed to begin with. Discovering her fate became so important to him, that it was now a prerequisite for moving on with his own. He held off on going back to work, shut himself inside, kept his sleeping to a minimum, and played detective.

Charlotte was 14 years old the first time she considered suicide. It started after her fascination with the flute, which grew into, like most teenage obsessions, an idea that this defined her. Charlotte \Char·lotte \'Shär-lət \noun − a person who spends her life playing the flute, period, no questions about it. This quickly grew into a realization that she lacked any sort of patience to learn music and its many complexities. She could play the flute as well as anyone who dedicated an entire year to it and she knew that if she spent the time and energy continuing with the practice, she might become quite good at it, but she would never be a prodigy. She could never be one of those people whose souls entwined with the instrument upon their first meeting, a marriage that somehow produced sounds unlike anything that anyone had ever heard before. At best, she could be Charlotte who played the flute, but never Charlotte who redefined it.

So, she gave up on the flute, divorced it, marriage over, which left her with an empty space in the dictionary next to her name. Charlotte \Char·lotte \'Shär-lət \noun − a person… She wasn't afraid of the empty space. It would be easy enough to fill it back in with a new obsession—a prospect that probably excited most people—but what was the point? If it is so easy to fall in love with an idea and even easier to have the weight of it crush you, then what's the point of anything? Is that life? A constant search for a nametag that fits and stays on? And for a moment, she wanted out. She just wanted to leave. She didn't hate life, wasn't holding on to some teenage grudge against it. She just saw little value in it. It left a green line around her wrist, where it had once been a silver bracelet.

She couldn't kill herself, though. Her parents needed her, not because she brought anything special to their lives, or contributed to bettering it—in fact she probably made it far more difficult—but because they knew she existed and with that knowledge came the intense desire for that fact to always remain true. The only way to escape living without causing a rupture in the lives that surrounded her would be to not matter to them at all, to make it as if she never was.

She could have run away, or made her family hate her, but that would have been the same thing, wouldn't it? It would cause the same grief to her parents that death would. She would have to keep on living. There was no way to disappear completely. While most people struggled to create a name for themselves, to make some sort of legacy, Charlotte decided to be nothing more than a shadow, or a specter in the room. People feared the idea that they may not matter, while she found it nearly impossible to wipe away the fingerprint her existence left on the world. No matter how introverted Charlotte chose to be, she couldn't keep from leaving traces of herself in the world around her. Once she was, she was.

As she got older, existing for her parents meant having to exist within other definitions of herself. Not dying also meant living as expected. She received good grades, graduated, went to college, and eventually met Brian, who was not the flute but was a perfect person to marry at that time. Her parents gleamed on her wedding day, so proud of their daughter who lived the life people were supposed to live. Eventually, as a married woman, she would talk to her parents less and less, and they would not be sad about this, because it didn't matter if she existed in their lives, only that she didn't die in it.

Married life began easily enough, mainly because Brian kept to himself as much as she did. They both seemed interested in doing what they were supposed to do and put little stock in enjoying each other or life in general. They worked, they cleaned, and once a month or so, they collided in bed for mechanical sex that only happened because it was what should happen in a marriage.

Two years in, everything eroded and Charlotte's isolationist views on marriage no longer worked for Brian. She began to sense resentment from him, which turned to anger, which led to fights. She hated fights, not because of the emotional aspects, but because they put her in a spotlight that she tried hard to avoid. The solution for Brian was sex, more of it, more emphasis on it, more emotion during it, or something along those lines. She was sure that was what he was after.

The other solution was divorce, but things don't progress that way in real life. In movies, a couple can have one big blowout and it spells the end of their relationship, but in reality, things don't change so drastically. Couples fought, and usually, they could tell right away that things were all wrong, but to admit so would also mean admitting defeat, admitting failure, and accepting that a certain amount of time was wasted. Instead of chalking up the loss, couples clung to it further. They wasted more time, reaping an even bigger failure in the hopes that one day they would wake up and none of the fights would remain, the traces of them all wiped up, and the relationship was the vision they had set for it. Divorce comes many years later.

Charlotte and Brian's fights developed more frequently until they melded into each other, the beginnings and endings overlapping, every fight becoming an extension of the last. Brian took to the habit of slamming things, throwing things, and cursing. After his fits, he would tell her he was okay, but in a voice that gave away the lie. She would cry and then hate herself for crying. Weak people cry.

Things were all wrong. She knew that, but it wouldn't stop her from keeping it going. As far as she saw, things were always wrong. It was how life was and how it was made to be, but you just kept doing it anyway. It's not like there was anything better to do.

While Brian recovered in the hospital, Charlotte spent most of her time in the waiting room, coming in for visits when it was allowed, but avoiding long stays so Brian could enjoy being alone. She drove home on off hours to make sandwiches or snacks and brought them back in Brian's thermal lunch bag.

When the hospital released him, she drove him home and helped him inside expecting to see their home as a new universe, a place where she had a little more freedom. She called his family in advance, telling them to give him a few days before coming to the house so he wouldn't be over-whelmed, but the truth was she didn't want to be over-whelmed.

Shortly after, she realized that Brian never left the attack. He kept himself at the bus stop, surrounded by smoke. In doing so, he forgot that she was there. She was a shadow. A ghost. The thought of it made her gulp in a large breath that penetrated her body and loosened her muscles. She had never felt such an overwhelming sensation of relief. It ravished her and it cleansed her all at once. She no longer mattered to anyone and there was nothing more beautiful than that. She had the freedom to die.

Brian answered the doorbell, his sister barreling in as the door opened and she wrapped herself around him.

"I'm so sorry you have to deal with this when you just got done dealing with another tragedy."

People kept saying that to him, as if they believed that tragedies stacked on top of each other. They do not. His mind reacted to one tragedy at a time, dealing with them in an order, not as a series of weights piling into something he couldn't bear. One tragedy at a time, and for now, that was still the bus stop. He didn't have the ability to deal with Charlotte's death yet, and for that, he felt sadness, but that sadness would be the only connective tissue between the two events.

He had continued with his riddle, searching for the woman who he determined did not die at the bus stop, but disappeared amongst the deathly fumes that wafted into the sky that day. His house did not feel empty with Charlotte gone, but instead, it felt more alive. It was not as if a person had disappeared, but a curtain had opened. The sun beamed through the windows and spotlighted the wholeness, the completeness of the house.

His sister spoke in bursts about funeral preparations, and Charlotte, and the bus stop bomber, and of course, her own life and husband, because a person can only intercede on another person's life for so long before they have to revert to their own and remind themselves why they care about anything. She sat down on the couch offering to help in any way possible, and Brian thought the best way possible would be for her to head right back to her own life and husband as quickly as she could. She looked up at him, waiting for him to confirm he heard her.

"I'll be right back," he said and then walked out the front door.

When he said it, he had meant it. He planned to slip out the front door just to catch his breath and then go back inside to deal with his sister. He would fake tears and distress, and he would feel guilty for having to fake it. That was the plan, until one foot started moving and the next followed suit. His sister had crashed into his house like a grenade and he needed to get away from the blast. So, he walked, unsure where he was going, but walking, nonetheless.

He ended up at the same place he went to every morning for the last week, and he supposed he always knew he was going there, but wanted to believe it was happenstance. He sat down on a bench and looked upon the horde of people waiting for their buses to arrive. He didn't see the Hispanic girl, just as he hadn't every other time he had come here. Over the last week, he would arrive a few hours earlier and leave a few hours later than when she was normally there, just in case she changed her schedule after the bombing, but each time she remained a ghost.

He supposed this could mean she did die in the explosion, but it was reasonable to assume that someone who survived it would change their routine and let their fear steer them away from buses altogether.

The bus to Walton arrived, a new number 8, continuing on with life, following the route as if a homemade bomb had never stood in its way. A few minutes later, the 15 clanged over the potholes and hissed to a stop behind the 8. The 15 to downtown/Tarrow St. opened its doors and the steps whirred as they lowered to the curb. Brian had watched his bus come and go for a week now, sitting and waiting for the spirit of a woman who probably no longer existed. Maybe it was the right day for it, maybe he wanted to expand his search, maybe it was the desire to get farther away from his sister's home invasion, but today, he decided to climb the steps and put his money into the electronic collector.

The bus had a way of creating an earthquake every time it hit a road that wasn't entirely smooth. It banged, bounced, and made a wave of bobbling heads within it. Each encounter with broken cement caused a trembling through Brian's body and his heart shook along with the metal shuttle. He felt trapped in the tin container's belly and his mouth dried up at the thought of his escape options. Maybe the boy did have cohorts. Maybe someone would try to copycat the crime. If a bomb were to go off, he would die. There would be no surviving it this time. He hit the cord, and a loud DING reverberated throughout the pod. The sound of it taunted him and he swore the other passengers were staring at him, internalizing their laughter. DING. ALERT. WE HAVE A TERRIFIED MAN ONBOARD.

The bus slowed in front of a brick plaza. The brakes hissed and moaned, and the front and back doors folded in on themselves. Brian stood up and exited the bus. He felt his back arch the way it did when he walked up the basement stairs in the dark and received a tingle of shivers, as if everything bad in the world was right behind him and gaining. He moved with purpose but paced himself so he didn't look like a lunatic amongst the shoppers who occupied the sidewalks. One foot. Two. Three. Fourfivesixseven… As he walked away, the bus moved forward and the gap between them grew. A sense of security enlarged within him.

He stopped and let himself catch his breath. He wasn't sure how long he had been holding it in. The bus continued forward in the direction of his normal stop, five blocks further up. He could see the tail end of the bus already a few blocks ahead and decided it was a safe enough distance to begin heading toward his destination. He walked, and when the bus stopped at a red light, so did he, keeping himself at least a block behind it at all times. It was like a foolish kid's game, but it made him feel safe.

Each time he stopped, he examined the storefronts lining the road. He had passed by them more times than he could count, but never paid them much attention. They were all small stores, mostly family-owned, quaint shops. They dressed up their windows with flowers, kitschy trinkets, or signs that poked fun at the local quirks. "New Englandahs have no Arse."

He was two blocks away. The bus hit a light, and he mimicked its stop. To the right of him was a clothing store for women. A circular metal rack housed blouses and spaghetti-strapped shirts on the front walkway. A sign above it announced SIDEWALK CLEARANCE ITEMS!

He looked in the window and saw a woman browsing through a rack of jeans, and he could tell from the back of her head and the flounce skirt she wore that he was looking at the Hispanic woman. She was more than just alive. She was out shopping for jeans. She was alive and living.

A bell dinged as he opened the door. The woman behind the counter and two women in the corner of the store glanced up at him and then went back to their own worlds, deciding there was nothing of interest outside of them. The Hispanic woman never took her eyes off the jeans, which he found to be an odd subject for her attention, since he'd never seen her in anything but flounce skirts.

He approached her slowly. He wanted to run up to her, to hug her, or lift her in the air, but his body seemed unable to comprehend what was happening. It was as if he had gone into shock. She was here, and this was real.

He reached out his arm and tapped her shoulder. She jolted around, startled. A scar streamed from her forehead, arcing at her cheek and resting at her chin. It was an odd scar, a delicate and clean line, slender and neat. How could a dirty and violent cloud of wreckage create such a beautiful work of art? It was as if God traced His finger down her face, leaving His mark with her forever. God. Not a teenage bomber.

"Can I help you?"

"You're absolutely beautiful." The words just rushed out of his mouth. There was no thought or preparation. He had pictured this moment but never planned for it. No matter how much he convinced himself she had lived, he had never truly believed it. The idea betrayed common sense. Yet, here she was, alive. What good was common sense anyway?

"Excuse me?"

She began to turn back to the jeans. She could have walked away or given him a frightened look, but she didn't. She just closed off and narrowed her world to a rack of jeans. Brian stood on the outside: a stranger at her door. He would have to knock again.

"I'm sorry. I don't know what came over me. It's just, well, I don't know if you remember me. You used to take the bus from Tanner's Switch. I did too. I saw you every morning."

He paused and waited for a reaction. If there was one, he didn't see it. Was she even listening anymore?

"Anyway, after the, you know… the bombing. I thought about it. How I always saw you there. I wondered if you made it out. It's just nice to see that you did."

She lifted her head back toward him and he felt a trickle of relief. It wasn't over yet, but she only turned her head; her body still twisted away from him. He put out his hand.

"I'm Brian."

She hesitated and then raised her arm slowly. They shook hands. It was a cold and stiff meeting of palms. After a moment, she released her grip and turned her head back to the jeans.

"I didn't catch your name."

"Eetzlucid," he heard as she continued to examine jeans. Her head stayed downward and away from him. He wondered if she had ever studied a pair of jeans so intently before.

"I'm sorry?"

She turned her head this time. It was a quick, sharp motion, and her eyes grew wide. "It's. Lucy." The words poured out slowly and clearly, as if she was speaking to a child.

Brian laughed. It burst from him, louder than he planned

for it to. There was nothing subtle in it and the other women in the store took note before returning themselves to their own worlds.

"I didn't say anything funny."

"I misheard you. I had thought you said your name was elusive."

She shifted the jeans over, sifting through each pair in quick succession. The metal hangers slid against the metal racks creating a sharp whining tone each time. It sounded like the unsheathing of a sword. It felt like it too. Each time, he waited for the fatal blow that would follow.

"I took the bus today, for the first time since the explosion. I have to admit, it was hard." He thought if he talked about it, she might realize she could talk about it to someone who understood.

"I take the bus every day. Same as always. The day after I left the hospital, I was right back on."

He wasn't sure why she would lie. He supposed she might not want to admit she was frightened. Maybe it embarrassed her. He stood at the bus stop for a week. He stood there for hours. She was a ghost. He knew she didn't take the bus, but he also knew it wouldn't be wise to mention that just yet. He was already on unstable turf.

Finally, she turned to him with her full body. The jeans were out of the way and he had her attention. She lasered her eyes directly at his, and it broke his concentration; he had to look away. Her hand came out again and it took him a second to realize what she was doing. He extended his and their palms met in the same cold and stiff marriage they had experienced just moments before.

"It was nice to meet you," she said and then shuffled around him, heading for the door.

"Wait," he said as he turned to follow her.

She thought the jeans were nice but expensive. Of course, she thought that every time she came in here on one of her breaks. She browsed, talked herself into some clothes, debated paying the higher price for the convenience of being able to get them here, then talked herself out of paying the higher price. She played this game with herself on every visit, and on occasion, she caved and lost the round; or won the round, she still wasn't sure which it was.

When the man approached her, she remembered him instantly. He was the Bus Stop Man. He wore dark gray ties with light gray shirts. It reminded her of those magic pictures that you had to look at with unfocused eyes to see the image inside the colors. Today he was wearing jeans and a tee shirt. He was unshaven and his hair was an inch or so longer. The bomb may never have stopped exploding on poor Bus Stop Man.

She could take a compliment. Men had been telling her she was beautiful since she was too young for them to be saying it to her in the way they did. She always appreciated it, but since the scar, the compliments came in two forms, and one of those forms told her an ugly secret about the man delivering it.

The scar took nothing away from her looks. She knew this and so did every man who laid eyes on her. It was just a thin line. Some men thought nothing of it and made their compliments in the same tone and manner they would have if the scar weren't there. Others, however, recognized that the scar took nothing away from her beauty, but assumed that she would be so fragile as to not understand this. They complimented her in a way where they seemed to be telling her they were willing to look past the scar. It was less of a compliment to her as it was to themselves, for being so open and willing to look past it.

That was how Bus Stop Man decided to talk to her. He

might as well have said, "I still think you're good-looking, regardless of your deformity. Isn't that nice of me?"

She placed her attention back on the jeans while the man garbled on about the bombing and his concern for her. Again, it was all about his tone. He spoke with self-congratulatory triumph. Look at me, the caring man. I was concerned for you and now you owe me. She never understood men who felt that a woman in their minds was a woman in their lives. It was as if they believed their thoughts were a cell in which to cage a woman. I never stopped thinking about you, so you must recognize how wonderful I am for this. We now have a connection. We are entwined, in mind and body.

She kept friendly with the man while he introduced himself and found some peculiar humor in misunderstanding her name. She hoped that her reluctance to remove her focus from the jeans would be a clue to the man that she wasn't interested in talking, but she gathered the stubbornness he possessed. This man believed they had a connection. He dreamed it to be so; therefore, it must be the truth.

He began to ramble about how frightening his bus trip was today. This man had never left the bombing, she decided. Many people did this. They face a tragic event, and while they talk about the injustice of it all, and how much it crushed them, they secretly yearn for it. They can't let it go. They talk about it ad nauseam. They need to keep living it. It was a tragic event, sure, but it was an event nonetheless. It gave their lives something to be about, something to give it meaning.

The truth is most people love a tragedy. They pretend to hate it. They tell everyone how terrible the event was, but internally, they are reveling in it. When the tragedy didn't happen to them directly, they injected themselves into the situation. This is why people love to tell others where they were when they found out about major catastrophes. Why would anyone care if you were in a classroom or an office building when 9/11 happened? They wouldn't, but people will tell their friends all about it anyway, because the tragedy gave them something to break their boring lives apart.

Lucy wasn't one of those people, though. She didn't look back. It happened no differently than breakfast and lunch did. A bomb blew up. She lived. Now she will continue to do so. Something twitched in her stomach and she had an urge to explain this all to the man. It moved up her lungs and burst out of her mouth like a belch. She told him how she still took the bus, every day.

She hated herself for saying it. She had no reason to explain anything to the man and she worried that talking would give him the inclination that she wanted to continue the conversation. Would he ask if she took the same bus? Would she have to explain to him that she now took the 12, because she moved in with her parents? Would she then have to delve further into the explanation to let him know that she did this, not for herself, but for her parents? That she wasn't afraid to live alone, but that they were afraid for her?

She was angry now, bursting at the seams furious, with herself, with the man, with the damn prices of the jeans. She took a moment to breathe, so she would remain cordial. She soaked in a gulp of calming air as she extended her hand to the man. They shook and she walked away. He shouted for her to wait and his footsteps pattered behind her as she walked out of the store.

As she traversed through the crowded sidewalks, the man followed. He wouldn't be able to accept that their meeting went the way it did. You were on my mind, now you must be in my life. She crossed the road about a block before the wedding boutique she owned, and as she did, she caught the man's shadow keeping pace with hers.

She pretended a BANG blasted behind her. Maybe it was a car slamming into the man, or another bomb exploding and tearing the boredom out of a new set of lives. It didn't matter what it was; a BANG was enough. A BANG is always a tragedy, isn't it? The man would probably be pleased to have a do-over with one of those.

The BANG was not there, though, just the gentle cacophony of car engines rumbling down the road, and the sound of shoes against pavement coming from Bus Stop Man. *We are entwined, please wait for me.* He would be expecting her to turn, for their eyes to meet, and for sparks to ignite. He would think this is how life should be. Unfortunately for the man, Lucy was not the type to look back.

This story stemmed from two concepts that I rolled into one. The first came with the title. I wanted to explore the aftermath of a tragic event and the actions and ideas of a victim that reverberate reverberates into more "attacks." After the bombing, it is Brian who blows up everything around him, and creates his own victims.

The second concept I wanted to explore was the idea of "predestination" when it comes to relationships. I always find the idea icky. Hollywood romances, music, and just general thinking seem to love the idea of "soul mates," but I find it unromantic. Two people destined to be together isn't sweet. It's boring and weird, and often creepy and dangerous. You've seen romances where the man tells the woman, "We were meant for each other," and it's supposed to be beautiful, but imagine that man uttering the same sentence when the woman is trying to break up with him. The idea that someone is owed to another is not romantic. The universe and the powers of the wind binding you should be viewed as horrific.

What I do find romantic is the idea that two folks can bump into each other in this bizarre and fucked up world and somehow desire to make each other happy for as long as that works, and I find it even more romantic when they give each other the leeway to exit when it becomes important for one to do so.

GLAWACKUS

Charles walked ahead of Auggie, dragging an axe in one hand, and holding a cup of Dunkin' Donuts iced coffee in the other. They hopped the stone wall along the side of their house and stepped through the shrubbery toward the downed oak.

"Alright. Let's see if we can pull this off."

His son chased behind. "But why are we doing it now? Winter's over."

Charles dropped the axe, sat on the carcass of the oak, and swirled his coffee around with the straw, enjoying the satisfying sound of the ice spinning around its plastic prison. "The internet said you want to chop firewood six months before you'll use it. Said, beginning of spring is a good time."

"It just seems like a lot of work," Auggie said.

Charles sat up and heaved the axe over his shoulder, surprised anew by the weight of the damned thing. "Don't you want to get good at this kind of stuff? Self-sufficiency. You and I have been spoiled, my friend. And the world is going to shit. I think it's good to learn the things we'll need to know if the country falls apart."

Auggie put his hands in his pockets and rocked on the balls of his feet. "Alright. I'm in."

Charles appreciated his son's willingness to get in the spirit of adventure. The boy showed incredible restraint through all of life's recent changes, never complaining when they moved away from the familiarity of Crantson, where he grew up, to the woodsy neighborhood in Tanner's Switch. He even accepted all of his dad's new personality quirks. Charles was well aware of how much he'd changed since he and Auggie's mother, Diana, split up, but his son just rolled with it all.

Charles kicked the tree. "Do you want first swing, or should I?"

Auggie smiled. "I'll do it."

A group of black birds squawked obnoxiously, and a light breeze trickled in from the forest. Birds. Charles should learn what types were native to the area. He couldn't imagine why he'd need to know that in a survival situation, but survivalists always knew that kind of shit, so it felt important.

His shoulders relaxed as his son took the axe.

"Okay, so you just gotta…" Charles mimicked the action of slamming an axe down on the dead oak. He had no special knowledge on the subject, and probably should have watched a few YouTube videos before coming into the woods, but it seemed pretty self-explanatory. Lift and slam down. Right?

Auggie wobbled as he lifted the axe over his head, almost falling over. Instead of taking the time to correct himself first, he brought the axe down full force as he stumbled, luckily avoiding any maiming injuries. The heel of the axe struck purchase, and it stayed embedded into the thick surface of the oak's trunk. It only went a few inches in, but it was enough to keep the axe in place after Auggie took his hands away.

Charles put his arm around Auggie's shoulders. "Okay, make sure you're solid on your feet before you swing it, and maybe don't pull it so far back over your head. I don't want you to decapitate yourself."

"I had it, Dad." His pale, freckly cheeks turned cold red.

"I know. I know. Just, let's be as careful as possible." Charles put a foot on the trunk and used both hands to rip the axe from its body. "Jeez. That sucker really gets stuck in there." He handed the axe back to his son. "One more go?"

Auggie gripped the throat of the axe handle and gritted his teeth.

"Wait!" Charles put one leg back. "Separate your legs like this and bring the axe up by your side."

Auggie did as his father instructed and brought the axe down hard. It landed solid and went in deeper than his first strike, but about ten inches from the initial cut in the wood.

"Hell yeah, kiddo. Fantastic."

Auggie smiled, showing off his braces. "Your turn."

"Okay, let's give this a go." Charles put his coffee cup down in a pile of twigs. His feet dug into the cold earth. The axe went up and he slammed it down with all his might. He lost his grip on the handle as the weapon edged into the body of the tree. Like his son, he missed the previous marks, creating yet another cut into the wood. At this rate, they'd be at it all day without ever separating a single piece of wood.

"Maybe this is a lot harder than it seems," he said.

His son nodded. "We can't learn everything at once. It's gonna take time."

Charles put his hand on his son's wild brown hair and scruffed it. "Wise words, bud. What do you say we retreat and go watch a movie?"

Auggie nodded excitedly. "Yeah. The Shining?"

Charles shrugged. "Sure." He sat back down on the oak, sighing. "I really thought we could do this. Feels like an entry-level kind of thing."

Auggie laughed. "Chopping trees apart? You thought that would be easy?" He sat next to his dad.

His father joined him in the laughter. "I guess I did." He put his arm around his son. At least he'd have a new memory with Auggie. Sitting out there in the woods and trying something new suddenly felt worthwhile, even if the attempt ended in failure.

"When we drove in yesterday, I saw some kids hanging out by the bridge on that main road. Think I can go hang out with them sometime?"

"Of course you can."

Auggie had friends in Cranston, where his mother lived, but he didn't have many. Mostly the type who played video games and Magic the Gathering all day and night. The kid never dated anyone as far as Charles knew. And never really talked about liking anyone, either. He was a chubby kid, freckly, and he had braces. If other kids were around, he talked softly, and his cheeks turned red when the attention turned to him.

Sometimes at night, Charles would knock on his son's door to say goodnight, and he could tell from the response that his boy had been crying. It broke his heart. A few years earlier, he might have come in and offered comfort, but knew at Auggie's age, his father's sympathy would only make the kid feel worse.

He knew his son hoped to make some special bonds with the kids in this area, and maybe that's why he agreed to move in with his dad instead of staying with his mother in Cranston. Maybe he hoped a fresh start would offer him new opportunities to make friends. Charles desperately hoped for the same thing and felt more than a little terror that the other kids might be cruel instead.

"Come on, let's head back in," Charles said. As they rose from their seat on the tree, something screamed. The high-pitched, horrific sound came from far in the woods, but it penetrated Charles' soul. The sound carried pain and terror within it, but also anger.

"What was that?" Auggie asked, eyes wide.

"I have no idea. Let's get the fuck out of here."

They both walked faster toward the stone wall.

The scream came again. It sounded human, the noise someone would make while getting murdered.

Charles and Auggie hopped the stone wall, ran across the wooden patio, and around the house to the front door. Once inside, Charles slammed the door and locked the deadbolt.

"That was creepy," Auggie said, laughing now that they were in the safety of their home.

Charles went to the sliding glass door by the patio and peeked out to see if something had followed them. Nothing had. He laughed now, too. "What do you think that was?"

Auggie shrugged, no longer interested.

"Do you think someone was getting hurt? Should we call the police?"

Auggie plopped onto the couch and grabbed the remote. "It was probably just an animal."

The morning sun reflected off the sliding door's glass, and Charles had to cup his hands over his eyes to see the far stretches of the yard. "You're probably right. It didn't sound like any animal I've ever heard before, though."

"We lived in Cranston. The only animals we knew were rats." And then, totally over the subject, "I know it's early, but can we have pizza rolls for breakfast?"

Charles laughed and moved away from the door. He opened the freezer, seeing the nearly empty shelves. A bag of fish sticks, another of curly fries, and two tubs of Ben and Jerry's. "I think we finished off the pizza rolls last night, bud."

"What else do we have?"

"Not much, to be honest. I should have grabbed some donuts when I hit the Dunkin' drive-through this morning."

Auggie's eyes lit up. "Can we do that now?"

Charles checked the back door again. Nothing. And he hadn't heard the sound again, not that he knew if he would within the confines of the house. "How about we go to Walmart and stock up on stuff instead?"

A few minutes later, they marched to the Mazda. Charles caught the neighbors next door sitting on their porch. He'd met them yesterday, and they had all done a round of introductions. Dave and Nancy. They'd lived in Tanner's Switch their whole lives and knew all the gossip Charles could want and a whole hell of a lot he didn't want.

He tapped his son's arm. "Hey, let's go chat with them for a second."

They strode across the two acres of yard separating their house from the neighbors, and waved when they reached the property line. "Hey guys," he said as he stepped onto their lawn. Dave and Nancy sat in rocking chairs drinking what looked like lemonade, and Charles found it quaint, the kind of thing he had envisioned for him and Diana when they got older.

Dave and Nancy waved. Nancy said, "How are you both settling in?"

"Well," Charles said, putting one foot on their front step. "Buy, hey, did y'all hear any screaming a little while ago?"

Dave and Nancy looked at each other with furrowed brows. Dave said, "No, sir. What kind of screaming?"

"It was loud," Auggie said.

Charles put his hands in his pockets. "We were in the woods over there, and it was this intense screaming. Sounded kind of angry, but also…"

"Maybe like a baby crying," Auggie added.

Dave sipped his lemonade and swatted his hand as if a fly were bugging him. "Sounds like a fisher cat to me. You'd hear 'em nice and early. They're crepuscular."

"Crepuscular?" Auggie asked.

"Means they come out at dawn and dusk." Dave took another sip of lemonade.

"So, fisher cats make that kind of horrible noise?" Charles asked. "I mean, it was really loud."

"Sure do. It's a terrible sound. Like your boy said, sounds like a cryin' baby."

"What's a fisher cat? Are they like normal cats?" Auggie asked. Charles loved how his son always thirsted for more information. He was inquisitive by nature, and Charles thought that was a fine way for a boy to be. Adults stop asking questions, priding themselves on 'figuring it out,' and that usually makes them grow dumber and dumber.

Dave put his glass down on the wooden porch. "No boy, a fisher ain't like a normal cat. They look like big-ass weasels. They usually don't mess with people, but if you do run into one and it feels cornered, it'll give you a nasty scratchin' and bitin'. But I'll tell ya, those things can scream. It's obnoxious, quite frankly. Sometimes it sounds like a baby crying and sometimes it sounds like laughing."

"So that's it then? Just a big weasel thing had us scurrying into the house? I guess we have a lot to get used to in the woods." Charles put his arm around Auggie.

"Oh yeah, you'll hear lots of types of screaming from the animals. Coyotes, foxes, even some owls. And don't even get me started on the bobcats. None quite as annoying as the fisher cat, though."

Nancy rocked in her chair. "Unless you heard a glawackus."

Dave laughed so hard he coughed. "A glawackus!"

"Is that some kind of fake creature the country folk trick city folk with?"

Nancy smiled. "Oh, nothing so mean. I was just teasing. The glawackus is an old myth from Connecticut. Used to be a lumberjack tale back in the 30s. Big monstrous creature in the woods who screamed and laughed before killing all the livestock, and maybe a few people on its way."

Dave pointed at Charles. "You should look it up. There's some fun stories with it. Local paper even had hunters stagin' with a fake creature. It was all the rage for a while. Some folks said it was a giant cat, others a lion. Some even went so silly with it they said it was a cat in the front and a dog in the back. This was all before our time, but the tales lived on well past our youth."

"Funny thing is, even the name was stupid. The 'gla' was for Glastonbury, where they were sighted. The 'wack' was literally for 'wacky' because the story was so dang dumb. And then the fool who named it added the 'us' at the end to make it sound all Latin and official."

Nancy said. "You got scary myths out there with names like Wendigo, Yeti, Loch Ness, and what do we get? Glawackus. Who's gonna be afraid of that?"

"Alright, well, we have to head to Walmart. Thanks for clearing it up for us. Expect screams in the morning and evening. Noted," Charles said.

Nancy waved as they walked away. "Have a good day," she said before she and Dave went back to chatting and laughing. Charles couldn't help but feel like the butt of the joke.

On the way to Walmart, they passed by a group of kids walking down 91. One of them had a basketball in hand, and the rest were all drinking sodas. Auggie stared out the window at them. Charles noticed but didn't say anything.

At Walmart, Charles told Auggie he could scope the video game section before they did their food shopping, figuring the kid could use some entertainment until they settled in and found a routine. Auggie had a PS5 with plenty of games, but Charles understood there was nothing like ripping the plastic off a new disc.

While Auggie went to the games, Charles hovered around the Blu-ray section, searching for a scary movie they could watch together. As he read the back cover of *Bunker Dogs*, the

Caleb Jones version, not the newer one where Kevin Bacon voiced the White Wolf, he overheard his son chatting with someone.

Peeking over the shelf, he saw a boy and a girl listening as Auggie talked to them about some kind of game. The lingo was beyond Charles' understanding, but the kids seemed intrigued, and Auggie looked excited, confident even.

Charles grabbed his shopping cart and moved away quickly, not wanting to ruin his son's vibe. He tossed *Bunker Dogs* into his cart and moved down a little further to the fitness watches. On a whim, he went to the electronics checkout to buy one. Nothing too expensive, but enough to keep him checking his steps.

Auggie caught up with him as he took his card of out his wallet.

"Hey, can I get this?" He handed his dad a game with a female clown fighting a hulking man lashing a whip. The title read Circus Wars VI. But the price tag read $24.99, and that was the important part for Charles.

"Hand it over to the man," he said, and Auggie nearly jumped for joy.

"Thanks, Dad."

He paid for the watch, the Blu-ray, and the game, and the two made their way to the food section. As they walked, Charles asked, "So, who were you chatting with?"

Auggie did a double take, catching on that his dad saw him with the other kids. "Oh, Crystal and Shawn. They seem cool. Shawn gave me his number. He said he has over 10,000 Magic cards. That's insane."

"That is insane. Those things cost a fortune. But hey, you made some friends before you even started school. That's pretty awesome, right?"

Auggie put his head down. "Yeah, but they go to Westerly, not Chariho."

Charles turned the cart toward the frozen section. "You'll still get to hang out with them after school, assuming you guys become friends enough for that."

"They gave me their gamertags, so I'll probably catch up with them in a game sometime. Why are you looking at frozen fruit?"

"I'm trying to eat better. Thought I might make some smoothies in the blender."

"I'll try one."

Charles tossed a frozen fruit mix in the cart. "We don't need to go crazy, though. Let's get some pizza rolls, too."

Auggie smiled. "Thank God."

On the drive home, they kept quiet. Auggie snacked on a Mr. Beast candy bar, while Spotify played the best of Bad Religion. Back at the house, Charles threw a frozen supreme pizza in the toaster oven while they unloaded the groceries.

"Dad, can I ask you a question?"

Stuffing bags of frozen food in the freezer, Charles said, "Sure."

"Why did you and mom split up? I mean, I know what you told me. Mutual and blah blah blah. But, like, someone had to bring it up first, right?"

Charles closed the freezer and leaned against the counter, wishing he had a blanket to crawl under and hide away from the question, and also maybe the whole world. "I guess you're mature enough to handle all the truth without casting judgment on either of us, right?"

Auggie shrugged, but his jawline tensed a little. "Of course. I love you both."

"I never would have gotten a divorce. I loved your mom, and I still do. But she was right. Once she said it all out loud, I had no argument. We weren't happy and hadn't been in a long time. And I'm pretty sure she stopped loving me years ago. Some people argue all the time, and others retreat into themselves. That's what we did. We didn't butt heads or fight. We just… drifted."

"But why? You're a good person. You always treated us well and you're a good dad."

Charles crossed his arms around his torso. "Sometimes being good isn't enough. And it's not fair to the ones you love to rely on that. Look, we all have aspirations. I wanted a nice family, a house, and to feel relatively safe. And I got those things. And the more I had them, the more I wanted to protect them, but I didn't protect them by actively participating. I protected them by sinking into them. Why go out when we're safe at home? Why do fun things when we can all watch movies and avoid all the problems in the world? Why risk anything? I just went to work, came home, and clicked on the TV until bedtime. And while doing that felt like wrapping myself in a warm blanket, it felt suffocating to your mom."

"So, she just wanted you to be more fun?"

He put his head down and laughed. "A little, sure. But it's bigger than just having fun. She wanted me to be lively. To show love. To lead sometimes. To act."

"But what's wrong with staying in and playing games and watching movies all day?"

Charles frowned. "Nothing if that's what you want. But it's not what your mom wanted. And if I'm being honest, it's not what I wanted. It's just the routine I set up for myself and the longer I did it, the scarier it became to break it. But it was also selfish, because by setting that lifestyle up and arguing against doing fun things, I took away from you and your mom."

"It's not like we never did anything. You took us to Bar Harbor. That was fun."

Charles checked the pizza through the toaster oven

window. "Yeah. I broke out of it sometimes, but rarely. And when I did, I usually dragged my feet on it until your mom pressured me to a breaking point."

"Oh. Is that why you keep trying to be outdoorsy now?"

Charles laughed. "Trying and failing. Yeah, it is."

"You think mom will take you back if you do?"

Grabbing an oven glove, Charles said, "No. Our relationship is done and gone, buddy. I don't want you to get your hopes up that that will change. I'm doing the outdoorsy stuff because your mom was right. I'm not trying to prove something to her. I'm trying to prove something to myself."

He took the pizza out of the oven and placed it on the counter. As he opened the drawer to find the pizza slicer, something banged hard on the patio. Both Auggie and Charles jumped.

"What was that?" Auggie said, hiding against the fridge.

Charles felt the raging rapids in his blood, the familiar course of adrenaline at any anomaly life had to offer. The screams in the woods were far away, and he could tolerate them for that reason. But something encroaching on his personal space pulled all the terror back.

One night, in Cranston, he woke up at two in the morning because he heard a noise outside. When he looked out the window, he found three teenagers walking down the road. They looked like punks. One of them peeked in a car parked in the road as he walked by it, and for weeks after, Charles struggled to sleep, wondering when someone would cross his property line and break into his car. That, of course, would only be the first step. Once a criminal entered the car, the universe would open the door for anything. When you give them a car window, they take the house next. And that meant his family wasn't safe.

Now, In Tanner's Switch, amongst the safety of the trees, trouble found Charles.

He put his finger to his lips and whispered for Auggie to

stay put. Peeking around the corner of the fridge, he glanced through the sliding glass door. At first, he saw nothing. Then he noticed it and turned red with embarrassment.

"It's just the axe," he said. "I must have left it leaning against the house and it fell over."

Auggie's eyes remained wide, and he kept himself pinned to the fridge. "You left the axe in the woods, Dad."

"It's okay, Auggie. I'm sure I didn't because it's right there. Do you think an axe murderer found it and what? Just tossed it on the deck?"

Auggie's pupils moved around as he considered this. Slowly, his body separated from the fridge. "I could have sworn you left it in the woods. I remember thinking it was a bad idea to leave it there, but we were both scared and ran inside, and by then I just forgot about it."

Charles pointed out the sliding glass door and Auggie brought himself around to see the axe lying still on the patio.

"Weird," Auggie said.

Bang!

Something else slammed against the window, spreading brown liquid all over it. Charles nearly fell over. His mind took a second to catch up. The instant the noise hit the house, he thought someone fired something at them. Then, when the liquid spread across the glass and dribbled down, he couldn't make sense of it at all.

"Hide!" Charles yelled to Auggie.

The boy dipped back behind the fridge.

Then, it registered. It was his coffee. The one he'd left in the woods with his axe when he and Auggie ran back inside. Because Auggie had been right. He'd left the axe in the dead oak. The house around him spun. Thump. Thump. Thump. His heartbeat blasted in his ears.

What should he do? Hide somewhere? Can you call the police about a rogue iced coffee cup? There had to be an explanation for this. Maybe a neighbor who lived across the woods saw him leaving his garbage behind and just expressed his frustration with a little too much gumption. Or maybe Charles left the cup… Where? On the fucking roof and it fell off? No. Someone definitely threw it.

He turned to his son. "Stay here."

Auggie nodded. Charles crept toward the glass. The coffee made it difficult to see through, and the late afternoon sun doubled the difficulty. Charles crouched down and looked through the glass where the coffee hadn't reached. He saw nothing in the yard, no crazed coffee-throwing criminal waiting with a horror movie mask.

A shadow passed on the left side of the patio, as if something walked along the stone wall. It was too low to be a human, which relieved Charles, but it was also too big to be most animals Charles knew of. Unless it was a bear.

The scream that followed shook Charles to his core, so high-pitched and volatile, he felt it deep within his bones. And then the shadow was gone.

Auggie sniffled. Charles pushed away from the door, hiding behind the wall next to it, and in a position where he could see his son, who stood shivering at the fridge.

"What the fuck?" Charles whispered.

"Dad, what is it?"

"I don't know."

"Is that a fisher cat?"

"I don't think fisher cats throw shit. And I know Dave and Nancy said they can scream really loudly, but that was fucking insane."

They stayed in their respective spots for about ten more minutes, and when nothing else happened, they slowly peeled themselves away. Charles ran to the couch, where he'd plopped his phone when they came back from Walmart.

"I'm calling the police."

"What do you think did that?" Auggie couldn't stand still, the nervous energy bursting into his limbs.

"Dave and Nancy."

"What? Why?"

"I don't know, but they told us a story about some big ass animal, and they were laughing at us, and then all this shit happens? Obviously, an animal can't throw coffee cups and axes. They're fucking with us."

"They're old, Dad. Old people don't play pranks."

"Old people who think of everything in 'us vs. them' do. People who live in towns like this don't like when city people come in. I see it on the town pages on Facebook all the time. They bitch about the 'yuppies' and 'snowflakes' moving in and changing their towns. They're fucking with us because they want us to leave."

"They seem nice, Dad."

"Auggie, I don't know. Maybe it wasn't them. But someone is fucking with us, and I want the police to check it out."

He dialed 911.

When the police arrived, they took him far more seriously than he expected, when his big pitch was, "Someone through coffee at my window, and I saw a cackling animal on our wall."

They scanned the area, even went into the woods a little, and talked to the neighbors to see if anyone saw anything. Of course, the only neighbors close enough were Dave and Nancy, who Charles thought might be responsible. He didn't tell the police that, though, because he had no real evidence to suggest they did anything. Of course, they didn't witness anything happening, just like they didn't hear a scream in the woods earlier that morning.

Charles thought the police would soothe his nerves a little, but as soon as they left, he was back to a ball of anxiety. Auggie seemed all right though. He dove into his new video game and ate his cold pizza. Charles wished he had a hobby to lose himself in.

To keep his mind busy, he put in his earbuds and listened to an audiobook while he straightened up the house. They'd just moved in, so there wasn't much to clean outside of the police footprints and some dishes, but he had a few boxes yet to unpack. His mind kept going back to the coffee, and every time he heard a subtle noise, he took an earbud out to listen closer. Half an hour in, and he had no idea what had happened in the audiobook.

With all the chores done, he decided to nibble on some of the cold pizza, his stomach finally relaxing enough for him to do so. Then, he put his earbuds away and sat next to Auggie.

"Maybe we should do the movie now?"

Auggie hit pause on the game, stood up, and slid *Bunker Dogs* into the PS5.

Before Cassie and James ran into the underground cellar, Charles fell asleep. And when he woke up, his world went to hell.

Auggie's scream woke him up, but if not for that, the window smashing would have done the trick. Glass splashed across the living room floor, luckily away from them. Charles stood up and grabbed Auggie, acting without thinking. His chest ached from the intense wakeup.

As soon as they were both on their feet, something came through the window, thudding hard on the glass-speckled carpet. At first, he thought someone threw another object at their house, but he quickly realized the object moved on its own.

It was huge, as long as an alligator, and as tall as a Great Dane. It spun with the slithery movements of a weasel and let out its horrendous scream. At this distance, the sound was deafening. Charles felt it in his spine.

Auggie screamed, too, and that didn't help Charles concentrate.

Thinking only of moving the creature away from his son, Charles jumped on the couch, away from his boy, and yelled, "Hey!"

For the first time, he caught the creature's face. It was cat-like, but its eyes weren't even. One hung lower than the other. And its mouth was littered with sharp, yellow teeth.

Charles hopped over the arm of the couch and headed toward the kitchen. He turned and walked backward to keep his eyes on the beast. He could smell it now, fish breath and wet towel fur. It crept toward him, its upper lips curled in a snarl.

Charles waved his hand toward the bedroom door, trying to get Auggie to run the fuck out of the living room. His son didn't listen, though. He just stood there, frozen.

Charles took another step backward, giving himself a view of the kitchen in full. He eyed the knives in the block. If the animal pounced, he'd never get to it in time. Trying not to entice the creature, he slid his feet back one painfully slow step at a time.

Keeping his teeth gritted, he said, "Auggie, get the fuck out of here."

Auggie snapped out of it and ran for the bedroom, which caught the creature's attention. It turned around with uncanny speed and snapped at Auggie, which caused the boy to jolt backward into the wall. Now the creature blocked his escape.

"Hey," Charles yelled, trying to steal the attention again. But the creature didn't listen. Instead, it slithered forward, right for Auggie.

"HEY!"

Realizing the creature had a new prey and wouldn't be

distracted, Charles ran for the block and grabbed the chef's knife. Auggie screamed again. When Charles ran out of the kitchen, he saw the blood. The animal's teeth were embedded in Auggie's arm, and it shook its head, ripping and tearing at the flesh.

Charles dove, landing on top of the creature. He brought the knife over his head in the same manner Auggie had with the axe, and then drove it down into the nape of the beast's neck. It let out that horrid cackling screech again and violently shook until Charles lost his grip and fell off the monster. It gnashed its teeth and snapped at Charles.

He brought his feet up defensively, and the monster bit right in, clasping its jaws around his ankle. The pain was instant and powerful. He'd never felt anything like it as the creature chewed through his skin and touched the bone.

Auggie roared a war cry and swung at the monster. Boom. Boom. Boom. Like a boxer, Auggie poured out a medley of punches. Jabs, right hooks. Unfortunately, however much power he packed into those swings, the creature appeared unphased.

It jerked its neck back and forth, digging its teeth in tighter. Charles slid across the room, back and forth.

"Auggie, the knife!"

Auggie's eyes widened, and he dove for the crimson-soaked weapon lying on the carpet. Glass crunched under the boy's body as he hit the floor. Before he could touch the knife, the monster whipped its head around and buried its teeth into the meaty part of Auggie's calf. Another scream, and a far more haunting one for Charles: his boy in pain.

Charles slid toward the knife, and again, the monster whipped its head, crashing its thick skull into Charles' face. Something cracked, and his vision turned red. With both hands, he rapidly brushed the blood out of his eyes to see his son. Nothing mattered more than protecting Auggie. While he struggled to see, screams enveloped the room, both from the creature and his boy. Charles' stomach twisted and squeezed.

"You motherfucker. You leave him alone! Where are you?" He wiped enough blood away to finally see a little. The room was blurry, but he made out shapes. The creature's head bobbed and shook. Auggie was somewhere in front of the monster, out of view. But his high-pitched screams made it clear the monster was chewing on him.

Charles kicked, hitting the thing in the midsection. It lashed, but Charles was ready for it. As the thing bit into his arm, Charles dug his fingernails into the creature's left eye. The monster yelped, and for the first time, it was a sound of gut-wrenching pain. The eye made a squelching sound and then a pop as Charles ripped his fingers out.

Auggie flopped to the floor.

"Auggie, stay awake," Charles yelled as he searched for the knife. He found it by his foot, grabbed it, and slammed it into the creature's ear. The monster's one good eye widened in surprise. Blood splashed all over the television set as Charles plucked the knife out.

The beast rolled onto its side, spitting venomous screeches into the void. Charles didn't know how much time he had, so he scurried to Auggie, his palms pressing into blood and glass. Auggie wasn't moving, just lying on his side, breathing thinly. Charles tried to locate the injuries, but so much blood covered the boy's skin, it was impossible to find where the bite marks were.

"Auggie, can you hear me?"

Something thumped behind him. He swung around, seeing the creature on its feet. Its tail whipped harshly, knocking the television off the stand. The crashing startled the beast and drew its attention away from Charles just long enough for him to lunge. The knife drove into the thing's ear again, and again, and again. Blood sprayed across the white walls. The creature dropped to its side once more, and

Charles used the momentum to roll the beast onto its back. He slammed the knife down between the thing's ribs and pulled down until the knife opened the creature, showing its insides.

Gore and blood poured from the animal, draining out like an overflowing bathtub.

Charles ran back to Auggie. Sirens blared, loud and vulgar like the monster's screams. Red and blue strobed through the windows.

"In here," he yelled, clutching Auggie on his lap. "In here."

The police barged through the door. Four of them. A young guy in shades covered his mouth at the sight of the creature. "What the hell is that?"

One of them saw Auggie and immediately got on his walkie.

Movement. So much movement. Talking. Too much talking. People moved in and out of Charles' sight. They asked questions. One of them went to work on Auggie. Soon, rescue people showed up, and they worked on him, too, before placing on a stretcher and bringing him to the ambulance.

As they wheeled him out, he caught Dave and Nancy staring from their yard. Nancy had her hands over her mouth in horror. Dave's skin was ghostly pale.

The ambulance doors slammed shut, and the ground crunched under the wheels as they left the scene.

Charles told the police everything that happened in as much detail as his hysterical mind allowed while he lay in a hospital bed, waiting to hear about Auggie. Whenever a nurse stopped by, he begged for updates, pleaded to see his boy.

Finally, a doctor came in and told him he could visit his son. Charles' leg was bandaged, as well as his arm. He had to use crutches to walk, but it didn't stop him from flying through the labyrinthine hallways of the hospital.

"Oh, Auggie," he said as he entered the room. His son lay on the hospital bed with the headrest up, where he'd been watching television. His eyes were black and blue, swollen so badly that his face looked like a blobfish. The beast must have headbutted him like it had Charles.

Auggie's arms were covered in stitching, his legs, too. Charles hated himself for each bite, that he hadn't done more to prevent them.

"Dad!" Auggie exclaimed at the sight of his father.

Charles hobbled over to his son and bent low for a hug. They embraced for a minute, which somehow got them into a laughing fit.

"Oh, Auggie, I'm so sorry."

"For what?"

"For not protecting you."

"But you did."

The door to Auggie's room swung open, and Diana rushed in, panic covering her face like a balaclava. "Auggie! Jesus. What happened?"

She cried at the sight of him and rushed to his side. "What happened?" she asked Charles, no accusation or hostility in her voice. Only worry.

Charles told her the story. The entire, unbelievable story. She took it in as best a person could and didn't, for a second, question any of the insanity. Probably because the story involved the police seeing the damned monstrous animal. She whimpered a few times at the more gruesome parts, and Charles himself nearly lost his voice telling them. During extreme stress, people tend to lash out, to get angry without reason, but Diana did none of that. The only accusatory comment she made was, "I knew he would have been better off in Cranston," but she took that back by the end of the retelling, and even apologized.

The three of them sat in Auggie's hospital room, flipping through the television and watching whatever crap they could find on the fifteen available stations. And for a brief time, it felt safe. It felt good. It felt like home.

But eventually Diana left after convincing Auggie to spend the weekend with her in Cranston. Again, there was no pull or fight about it. She wasn't trying to lure him back. She loved her son and trusted him to make the decisions best for his life. She just missed him and wanted to be his mother while he was hurt. Charles worried he'd visit her and never come back, but he felt the same way Diana did. Auggie could choose what he wanted, and Charles would never make the kid feel bad about it.

Once Auggie's mother left, the weight of responsibility collapsed on top of Charles again. It was hard to be alone, to know the person he loved the most relied on him to make it all work, to protect, to keep the ebbs and flows of life natural and without flooding.

Charles wondered if he was responsible for the monster. If a person plugged a leak in the ceiling with tape, they're just blocking the water from dripping down. It would still collect up there. Eventually, it would build up so much, it would collapse and rain inside the house. For all these years, Charles had plugged holes and let the water grow and grow until it poured down in the form of a fucking demon cat.

At midnight, Charles cried to himself while Auggie snored.

At two, Charles cried again.

At four, he finally fell asleep too.

In the morning, they called an Uber and headed home. A heavy stone pulled on Charles' guts the closer they drove to the house. He didn't want to see the mess, the blood, the remnants of horror. The house itself would be exposed from the shattered window. Maybe bats had flown in overnight, taken over the living room. Maybe more Glawackuses. Was there more than one?

Charles knew some questions were best left unasked, but he couldn't stop himself. "Do you think you'd feel safer in Cranston?" He didn't want his son to have to muster the courage to leave. He wanted Auggie to know his father understood.

"Why?"

The Uber driver turned onto their road. "Well, to get away from whatever we just dealt with."

"There's monsters everywhere, Dad."

That was true, he supposed. There were monsters everywhere. The car pulled into the driveway, and Charles couldn't stop looking at the broken window, a gaping invitation for trouble, a wound, an infection.

There were monsters everywhere.

I grew up in the city, and for most of my life, I aspired to live in bigger cities. I never envisioned a country life, or a quiet one. Noise! I love noise. If you've met me at a signing, you can see that in my obnoxious personality. But as I grew older, I retreated to a more quiet, peaceful area, and now the city terrifies me.

I've noticed from town pages and various other places that the folks in these small towns do not like city people moving in. We vote differently. We envision different futures. We step on their toes and bring with us all the things they try to keep out. I personally don't care what they think, but I see it nonetheless. Most of those people are all bluster online, but some of them are truly hostile to anyone they perceive as an outsider.

I wanted to put a little of that into a story without it becoming a Deliverance-style mocking of country folk. Instead, I wanted to focus on our newcomers and them dealing with their own problems.

Charles thinks moving somewhere new and acting differently will fix his life's problems, and Auggie, too, hopes a new environment will provide him with a better life, but often times we just carry our problems with us, and pick up some new ones on the way. That's not to say a change of setting can't be beneficial. Auggie does meet some new friends, and while Charles didn't learn to cut his own firewood, he put some effort into something, and I gather he'll continue to do that. And together, they fought a monster.

Most importantly, they learned you can't run from monsters. They're everywhere. And you just have to keep facing them.

The Glawackus, by the way, is a real Connecticut legend.

BROCK HESFORD: FILM CRITIC

When Brock was six, back when his father came home from work in the evenings and took the occasional day off, the two of them went to Tanner's Switch Community College to surprise Brock's mother with a lunch break visit. Brock's father tucked a paper bag filled with chocolates and a sandwich from Donatello's Deli under his arm, and with his other hand, he guided Brock up the steep parking lot toward the entrance ramp. The building, brutalist and drab, felt so massive, so imposing, so dangerous. He wondered how his mother swallowed the gumption to enter it every day.

Clustered around the ramp, a group of college kids with signs shouted at everyone passing by. They yelled about a war, but Brock was too young to understand what it all meant.

A girl with thick, black eyeliner, eyes red and stormy, broke free from the mass of shouting students and eyed Brock as he and his father approached the ramp. At first, Brock flinched, thinking she would yell at him the way the other students were screaming at everyone else.

As she got closer, Brock's father switched the paper bag to his other arm and shuffled Brock behind him to get the boy away from the nearing girl with the hurricane eyes. She bent down to Brock's level and tilted her head toward Brock's father, waiting for approval to speak to the boy.

None came, but Brock's father stopped walking, which the girl accepted as an invitation. She ran a finger down Brock's cheek, and his father pushed him away again, but Brock resisted his father's protection. Everything about the girl terrified him, and even at six, he knew those eyes spoke of something unstable. But the finger down his cheek shot electricity into his bones, and he wanted more.

As she spoke, the stench of cigarettes wafted in Brock's face. "You are a star," she said. Her head listed as she examined him, and those red-swimming eyes sparkled, little fireworks in a crimson sea. "You are a star born from the dust of an explosion in space, and you, my friend, have been bursting ever since."

"Okay, let's go," Brock's father said as he pulled his son forward, away from the anxious crowd. As they ascended the ramp toward the entrance, Brock looked back. The girl remained crouched, staring at him, eyes no longer sparkling. She smiled at him and waved the way adults wave at children, where they just open and close their fingers without moving the trunk of their hand.

Inside the building, the door shut, and the girl disappeared into memory. Brock's father took them up an elevator and down a series of long halls until they reached Brock's mother's office. They all hugged, and his mother said it was a wonderful surprise. The next half-hour both of his parents chatted to each other and to him, but he heard none of it. All he heard was, "You are a star born from the dust of an explosion in space, and you, my friend, have been bursting ever since."

Brock never stopped hearing those words. He was a genius, or that's what they called him. His teachers jokingly titled him "Doogie Howser." But his intelligence was analytical, utilitarian. He didn't have the patience or time for cliché meme philosophy, or cheesy expressions of hope and life and blah blah, saccharine phooey. He wanted it real, please. But for some reason, he accepted the nonsense spewed from a drunk college girl many years ago. "You are a star…"

Growing up, his hyper-intelligence pushed him into empty cafeteria tables, alone with the shadows on the playground. But those words always accompanied him. "…born from the dust of an explosion in space."

When his father took a new job that shipped him all over the continental US, keeping him away from his son for weeks and sometimes months at a time, the girl's speech rattled in Brock's brain like a handful of sandy seashells, sprinkling it with fine grains of nonsense. "…and you, my friend, have been bursting ever since."

Through his grandmother's death, his mother's stint in the depression unit of a psych hospital, and his father's brief visits, Brock clung to those words.

And now, too, as Tony pinned Brock's arms to the slick ice in Mr. Durgin's driveway while Angela Lamb smashed snowballs in his face, he closed his eyes and pictured the girl saying those words to him. Seven years later, he could still smell the cigarettes on her breath, and he could see the storm in her eyes.

You are a star.

Boom! A snowball exploded against his cheek. Its icy form felt like it cut into his red, raw flesh. Barry Ryan stood atop a snow mound at the top of the driveway where the plow had piled it. As Angela packed a new snowball, Barry kicked snow from the top of the mound, letting it rain down on Brock. He did all he could not to cry.

In movies, the bully is always clearly defined: an irredeemable menace, usually one with a couple of ugly henchmen, but Brock found this untrue to his junior high experience. Everyone was a bully, and everyone was bullied. It was just one clusterfuck of fear, hate, anger, and desperation that sometimes avalanched into a giant snowball to the face.

He could go weeks without an assault, without a single mean word uttered in his direction. Then, one day, someone would crack wise, or trip him, or throw used gum in his hair. But every once in a while, the perfect storm hit, and one person's aggression egged on another until three or four of them were heightening their attacks so as not to be the next in line for a bullying. Today, Angela started it, smashing a tightly packed snowball as hard as a construction helmet into Brock's face.

As laughter brewed, Tony and Barry joined in, eager to style themselves in the fashion of bully over bullied.

"What the hell is he saying?" Angela asked.

Tony leaned down, using his knees to keep Brock's hands in place, and tilted his ear toward Brock's mouth. "I'm a star? Something about bursting?"

"He's a fart? A bursting fart?" Barry said from the top of his hill.

Angela shook her head and pushed Tony off Brock. "Alright, let's leave him alone."

Brock stayed there for a while, letting the crunch of the other kids' feet on snow dissipate into nothing before sitting up. He never knew when they might change their mind, so it was best to wait until they were far away.

Brock didn't hate them. Didn't dislike any of them. He was an emotional kid. His intellect didn't deter him from feeling depressed, or sad, or overwhelmed, but he never let his emotions invade his reasoning. While, yes, his teachers called him Doogie Howser, and his parents boasted about his mind, Brock didn't think he was particularly intelligent; he just had a rationality that most kids don't possess. Heck, most adults didn't anymore, either.

He wiped the snow off his shirt and pants and used his sleeve to dry his face. The sharp, cold wrinkles on his jacket hurt as they hit his raw, wet flesh. When he turned the corner around Mr. Durgin's house, Angela was waiting, back against a bare oak tree.

"You alright?"

Brock's mouth turned dry. His heart hydroplaned as if it were driving on the icy roads. "Yeah, I'm fine." He didn't know if this was the right answer. Maybe she'd want to complete the job if he felt fine after the assault.

"You sure? That went a little too far. I'm sorry. I just wanted to be funny, and it just went too far."

It, he thought, *was a convenient replacement for I.* Just one extra letter, and the blame shifts.

"Yeah, I'm okay. I know you were all just playing." He kept walking, unnerved by the idea of having his back to her, but equally as unenthusiastic to stick around.

"Cool," she said, and went on her way. From the sound of boots on snow, Brock could tell she was going in the other direction.

He marched on, his heart cooling to the frigid air with each new step. When he took the turn to his street and saw his familiar blue house with the flacking paint, he wept at the sight. His sanctuary.

His mother noticed something was wrong the second he stepped in. "What the hell happened?" She dropped the television remote and ran to him.

He sighed. "Nothing. Please don't worry about it, Mom."

She scoffed as she put her warm hands on his cheeks. "You know I can't do that."

"I know, but there's really nothing to worry about. Just some kids being stupid. One of them even apologized afterwards."

She ushered him to the couch, and as she sat, she patted the seat next to her, signaling for him to sit. When he did, she put her arm around him, placed her hand on his cheek, and pulled his head into her shoulder. "You know you are loved, right?"

He chuckled. "Of course, Mom. I'm not upset. I promise. It's just shit that happens."

"Watch your mouth, but also, that's good to hear. It hurts my soul that anyone would want to hurt you."

He shrugged. "We hurt each other by existing."

"Well, that's bleak."

He swallowed hard. "Is Dad still coming home tomorrow?"

She nodded. "Said he's bringing, *'On a Clear Day, You Can See Block Island.'*"

"Awesome. Can't wait to watch it with him." He pried his head off his mom's shoulder, feeling a brick of lead in his chest at the removal. "You mind if I go up to my room now?"

His mother scruffed his hair. "Go."

For the last however many years, when Brock's father returned home, he brought a movie for them to watch together. Brock's transition from kid's movies to a more mature viewing happened on one of those visits, when his father plopped him down to watch the indie drama *Make Waves,* which was set in their hometown of Tanner's Switch, Rhode Island. At first, Brock complained. He wanted cartoons, dammit, but the movie involved a family with two mischievous kids who provided the hour-and-a-half film with some kid-friendly humor. Brock was entertained enough. But Brock's biggest memory of watching the movie was when his father would tilt toward his boy and whisper little tidbits, talking to his son as a peer instead of his little child.

"I used to go the beach that's in this scene all the time with my family growing up."

"Do you see the way this is shot with the camera up high looking down? That was done to establish how small the characters feel in this moment."

"Look at the way the camera pulls back, making it look

like the characters are moving away from the background. He's showing how isolated they feel from their surroundings."

Brock listened to each tidbit his father added, even when he didn't understand them. After the movie, when his parents went to bed, Brock looked the film up online. While he understood some of the humor and got the basic plot, he couldn't piece together the point of the thing. A family moved to the beach, and the parents fought, and the kids acted up, but nothing else really happened.

He thought the internet could provide answers. And it had. From Roger Ebert. "A character study," he had called it, which Brock took to mean, who gives a shit about plot when we have such interesting characters. Ebert gushed about the film, and Brock thought the review was not only more entertaining than the movie, but also an artistic display of its own. Ebert had mentioned a lot of his father's points but poured them all out in easily digestible descriptions.

From there, Brock looked up other reviews by Roger Ebert and wrote down a list of movies he wanted to watch based on the reviews. There was a misconception from folks about what a reviewer does. They thought a reviewer told you what to watch and what not to watch, but a good reviewer wasn't attempting to do that. They were telling you what THEY enjoyed or didn't enjoy about a movie. You weren't supposed to agree with them all the time, but the good ones gave you enough criticism to make an informed decision.

That's what the good critics did. But the great ones, the true legends of film review, they told their own story. Their reviews dissected and explored the film in such interesting and unique ways that their review was almost a special piece of the movie itself, intertwined in some subconscious way.

Brock tried to write his own reviews but dove so deeply into the terminologies, trying way too hard to "get it," that his reviews were bogged down by pretention. No one in the history of cinema wanted to read about a film's mise-en-scène. Ever.

But most importantly, he had found a connection with his father when the man showed up for his short-time stays. Brock used the list of reviews to recommend flicks for his father to bring home, and his dad would light up that his son found an interest in cinema. Throughout the movie, they'd discuss their opinions. Brock's father shooting from the hip, and Brock firing back with ammo handed to him by the online reviews he'd devoured before the viewing.

Too bad Ebert had passed away, because whenever his father suggested a newer movie, Brock had to find other sources to help him understand the movies, and no matter what, none of them lived up to Ebert's standards, not even the ones writing on his website since his passing.

Besides Ebert, Brock had one other "hero," and it was the director of *Make Waves*. About two years into his new hobby of reading movie reviews, Brock's father told him he was bringing home a new movie called *Cranston Angels*. When his father messaged him in their online chat, he stressed that the movie was directed by Karl Latos.

Brock remembered the name, but couldn't quite place it, so he went to Wikipedia. As soon as he saw the director made the very first movie that started his love for cinema, he knew he was a fan of the guy, and maybe Brock even changed his opinion of *Make Waves*. After all, if a movie wasn't valued for its place in a person's individual history, what was the use of entertainment anyway?

Better, though, Karl was a local guy. He grew up not more than twenty minutes from Brock. In an interview with *Rolling Stone*, he said he was a misfit growing up, always a loner, stuck in his own head with his art. They were connected, Karl and Brock, one and the same.

After the critical success of *Make Waves*, Karl didn't direct another movie for a few years, when he finally released

Cranston Angels, which received the same level of critical accolades, but just like his first film, didn't meet the commercial success the studios had hoped for. Brock already knew the theater-going audience was wrong for not seeing it, even if he hadn't watched it yet himself. The critics raved about it, and based on Karl's debut, Brock knew the man was a master at his craft.

After his father showed him *Cranston Angels,* Brock found Karl on Facebook and sent him a message. Brock wanted to make sure he didn't gush, coming at his new favorite director like a weirdo, but he wanted to stress his appreciation.

He went with: "Hello, Mr. Latos. I am a 13-year-old from Rhode Island. I live in Tanner's Switch, so not far from where you grew up. I have seen both of your films now, and I wanted to let you know they have inspired me to consider film as a career option for myself. Maybe I'll direct, too, or be a DP or something. I definitely want to work on the artist side behind the camera. Anyway, I just wanted you to know how much your work has meant to me."

He thought the message sounded normal and mentioning a "DP" showed that Brock knew a little about how a film was made. He wasn't just some dork pretending he wanted to get into an art form he didn't understand at all.

A few minutes later, those three little dots came in and out, showing Karl was actually responding. Brock spun in his chair, a ball of anxious energy.

"Hey, that's so great to hear. Kids usually want to be actors, stars, and don't take the time to understand how a film is made, so that was cool to read from you. ~~I~~ I appreciate you reaching out and letting me know my films meant something to you. Too bad the rest of the movie-going world doesn't see things how you do!"

Brock responded furiously, clacking hard on the keyboard, ~~and~~ letting Karl know the movie world was made of fools if they didn't check out *Cranston Angels*.

Karl responded back, and Brock back to him until the moon descended and a full-fledged conversation had brewed between a boy and his new hero.

It was worth the exhaustion Brock felt the next day at school.

That first conversation happened over a year ago, and Karl's third movie had just left the theaters. Brock wanted to see it on the big screen, but his father begged him to wait until he could bring it home on DVD for them to watch together. Brock's relationship with film came from his dad, so he chose to wait, lest he betray the foundation of his fandom.

That third movie was called *On a Clear Day, You Can See Block Island,* based off a book by some unknown Rhode Island author. And his mother had just informed Brock that his father would be bringing it home to them tomorrow night.

Once in his room, Brock flung his water-logged clothes off and changed into PJs before prying his laptop open and pulling up Facebook. He scrolled to Karl's name in his message list and typed: "My dad said he's bringing home On a Clear Day tomorrow! I'll finally get to see it!"

Karl and Brock had stayed in touch throughout the last year, although the conversations never reached the rapid back-and-forths they had on that first night. Brock understood. Karl was a busy man with a new movie.

On a Clear Day was his third film to escape a strong audience reaction, but worse, it had middling scores from critics as well.

Brock didn't care. He knew he'd love it. You aren't supposed to always agree with the critics.

He waited around the laptop for a while, but Karl hadn't responded, so Brock relented and went downstairs for dinner. While he ate, his mother chatted him up, trying to find out more details about what happened on his way home from school. He gave her enough nuggets to satisfy without giving her enough to storm the school tomorrow. His mind remained on his messenger, though, long since forgetting the snowball attack. He hoped Karl saw the message, and if the man was struggling with the reception of his newest movie, maybe he'd find some solace in knowing his biggest fan would be watching it tomorrow.

After Brock did the dishes, he ran back to his room, but Karl still hadn't responded. Maybe he was on a press tour or something.

Brock shut the laptop and went to bed. Tomorrow, school would be hell, and then he'd have his dad, his movie, and his favorite director.

The first half of Brock's school day went easy. No one bothered him or talked to him at all. All was fine until lunch, when Brock decided to forego his sandwich and apple for a trip to the library. He hopped on a computer and checked his messages.

Prepared for disappointment, his eyes lit up when his chat box with Karl's name was blinking. He knew Karl would be so happy to hear his biggest fan was about to see his newest film.

When he clicked the box, it opened to reveal: "Cool!"

Cool?

C-o-o-l?

That's all he got? Cool? He took a breath, reminding himself that Karl was probably busy working on another movie, although IMDb didn't have him listed for anything new. Or maybe he was still doing a press tour or something. Do those still go on when the movie hits DVD and streaming services? Probably not. Especially when the movie tanked in theaters.

But what the fuck did Brock know? Maybe Karl had big meetings with screenwriters or agents, planning out his next release. For all of his studying of the film industry and movie making, Brock had no idea how the folks inside actually operated.

Bang!

Something hit Brock so hard in the back of the head his vision went blurry, and his forehead slapped into the computer screen. The pain came and went quickly, but his nerves fired on all cylinders, and he knew they wouldn't quell for a while.

He turned to see Barry holding a thick book in his hands, wielding it like a baseball bat.

Brock turned back to the computer screen. He worried Barry would do it again but thought any type of engagement would prolong the assault. Let the jerk hit him a few more times and go on his way.

Barry didn't hit him again, though. He just said, "Fucking loser," and left. Sometimes bullying was intimate. Personal. There were true feelings wrapped up in the attack, usually misguided and projected feelings, but feelings, nonetheless. And sometimes they were fleeting aggressions just for the sake of them. Barry had no witnesses to revel in his cruelty. No friends to laugh with him. He didn't continue to attack with angry fists. He just hit Brock because he could and because he wanted to.

To Brock, that felt more like an adult cruelty. Kids are mean for reasons. Adults are mean because it's the only way to feel like they are real, tangible beings on a planet of humans who don't care about them.

Brock responded to Karl. "Thanks! I'm so excited to see it. I read some reviews, and I think it's going to be as perfect as Cranston Angels. You're a genius Karl and one day you'll be winning an Academy Award. I know it. Anyway, I know you're busy and haven't had much time to talk lately, but hopefully we can have a conversation soon."

Brock closed his computer, stretched, and headed toward the restroom. He hated public restrooms, and not because of how gross they were, although that too, but because of how hollow they felt, how echoey they were. It felt like being trapped underwater.

As he washed his hands after taking care of business, the door swung open, a gliding bird slamming into a wall. Barry stood on the other end. His eyes had changed. They were cold, cavernous things, as hollow as the restroom.

Brock's heart went into overdrive. He'd never encountered this type of situation. They always happened in the movies, but in Brock's world, the bathroom was sacred, even for bullies. People just did their thing and left.

But Brock knew that would not happen today. Barry found a bloodlust yesterday as he stood on that mound of snow. Maybe he regretted kicking piles of dusty cold onto Brock while the rest smooshed and smashed hard ice balls into his face. He had squandered his opportunity to make his violence lasting.

"Hey, Barry," Brock said.

Barry nodded and went to the urinal. Brock's shoulders dropped the weight they'd been holding, but he wasted no time in trying to get the hell out of there. As he made his way to the door, Barry turned around sharply and grabbed Brock by the neck, slamming him into the wall.

"What are you doing? What did I ever do to you?" What a stupid thing to say, like cutting his finger and dripping blood into the water for the shark to lick up.

Barry clenched his teeth. A vein on his forehead pulsed. He punched Brock in the stomach. Brock gasped, unable to breathe. The shot ripped the air from his body. It was like he was suffocating. He tried to move his arms up to fight Barry off, but before he could, boom boom boom. Barry punched him three times in the face.

The shots came rapid fire, and it took a few seconds for Brock to understand what had happened, for the pain to hit. By the time all the pieces coalesced in his brain, Barry had dropped him, left him alone. The door to the bathroom banged shut.

Brock covered his face and something warm and wet hit his hands. He pulled them away to see. His fingers trembled. Blood coated his palms.

"What the fuck? What the fuck?"

He looked in the mirror. His vision was messed up, cloudy on one side. When he looked in the mirror, he nearly fell over, nearly forgot his own body, and floated away. Blood gushed from his lower lip and nose. His cheeks were comically swollen, balling out like he had billiard balls stuffed inside his mouth. One eye was forced closed by angry masses of flesh surrounding it.

He screamed. Not a fearful scream. Not even an angry one. A lost one. An "I am so unsure what just happened and what the fuck to do about it" scream. Like someone lost in the woods realizing they won't make it home before dark. A scream begging for help, for understanding, for sanity to return. How could he ever face this? How could he ever return to school? How could ever feel comfortable around strangers? Around other humans outside of his household? How could he survive this? This wasn't the real world. Things like this didn't happen. The world was full of assholes and bad people, but there was an order to it. A rationality.

He stormed out of the bathroom into the desolate halls. Somewhere during everything the bell had rung, and people had made their way to their next classes. Now the hallway was just a long, hollow throat, and Brock ran down it, ran until he reached the double doors that would drag him into the belly of hell each and every day. He slammed his palms into the bar, and the door clicked, shot open, revealing the brightly blinding day with the sun prominent in the sky, reflecting harshly off the snow.

He squinted with the only eye that could squint and jog-walked. He wanted to run, but the ground was slippery.

Shivers drove up his spine thinking of the looming, grotesque building behind him, the place where horror happened.

The trip home was a blur. He didn't remember turning down Cobalt Ave., didn't remember Mr. Durgin's house, didn't remember the wind, or the cold, or cars passing by, but he did remember it being impossibly long, as if the streets stretched to mock him, to make his journey more ludicrous.

He came home to an empty house, dark and warm. It would have eased him if not for knowing he'd have to face his parents with a mangled face. His mother would worry. His father would pretend to, but Brock would see the disappointment on his face, the wish his son wasn't such a target.

He took a shower, washing the blood away. His eye already showed signs of black and blue. His cheeks hurt the most, and he worried a bone might've broken. The last thing he wanted was to lose the night with his father because of a hospital visit.

After he cleaned up, he decided to call his mother, ease her into what she'd eventually see. She picked up after two rings.

"Hey, why are you calling from the house phone?" The worry already hovered over each syllable.

"I didn't feel good, so I came home." He backtracked, unable to tell her exactly what happened.

"Oh, okay. Are you okay?"

"Yeah, I'll be fine. Just wanted to let you know."

"Listen, while I have you. I have some bad news. Your dad isn't going to make it home tonight. He said he will be back by the weekend, though."

"Wait… What? No. He has to come home tonight."

On the other end of the line, there was a bump and a clack, as if his mother was toying with the receiver. "He's sorry, bud. He wanted to be there too."

Before Brock could object, she poked a hole in his story. "Wait. Why didn't the school call me?"

"He has to come home tonight. He has to. I need him to." His voice broke. It was no longer a matter of seeing his father, or the movie. In fact, both would be better if his father did take a few extra days so Brock could go to the hospital, get himself healed up a little first. But this was bigger than that. The world was turning against him. Everything aligning to fuck him up.

"Brock, why didn't the school call me? What's wrong? What happened?"

"Mom. Stop. I'm fine. Why can't Dad quit his job? There's a million jobs he could take in town."

"We can talk about this later. Why didn't the school call me? Tell me, Brock. Or I'm coming home."

He slammed the phone down, picked it back up, and called his father. He got the voicemail. "Dad. What the hell? You have to come home. You have to. I don't care how, just please come home." The tears flowed. He couldn't help it. Everything inside him broke out, unleashed, as if his bones had been a cage for all of his emotions, and they'd shattered with those punches in the bathroom. Some of them may actually have done that. "Please. Just quit your job. You don't need it. But I need you. Please come home tonight."

He hung up and the phone instantly rang. The caller ID showed his mother's number. She'd be home soon; the events at school, the ones he'd tried to run so far away from, would come back. He'd have to explain them. He'd have to face the potential broken bones. Maybe a concussion. He'd have to deal with it, and he didn't want to deal with it. The principal, the police, who knew what would happen next, but Brock could sense those punches coming back at him as he imagined his mother running down that ramp and opening her car door. As she hit the gas and flew home. Punch. Fucking punch punch punch.

He screamed again, this time with agitation. After pacing a few times, rubbing his fingers on the tender wounds, he opened his laptop. No new messages from Karl.

"Karl! Looks like I won't get to see your movie until the weekend now. My dad can't make it home."

To his surprise, the three dots showed up a minute or two later. His heart raced with anticipation. Maybe today would have one sliver of goodness to it.

"Hey, kid. I want you to know I appreciate how much of a fan you've been, but I have to end this conversation. I hope you keep watching my movies, and I hope to run into you one day so I can give you some signed editions or something. I just don't think it's a good idea for a guy my age to be chatting with you online. Hope you understand my dude. You're an awesome kid, and one day maybe you'll be the one winning an Academy Award."

Brock read it three times, trying to understand it, hoping he'd misread something. "Karl. It's not a big deal. It's not like you're a pervert. You're just my friend. We've already been talking for over a year."

He hit send, but wished he hadn't, should have thought up something better to say, but this was an emergency, a flood pouring into his life, and he needed to bucket out some of the water before he drowned, and his mother would be home soon to add another deluge.

The three dots came up. *Please*, Brock ~~though~~ thought. *Please let something go right.*

"I know that. You know that. But it's a weird time, man, and there's lots of weirdos out there. I don't need something else going against me right now. We're still friends, little man. Just can't be chatting on social."

Brock couldn't breathe. He was losing himself, and he knew he was losing himself, and usually when this kind of thing happened, he stopped himself, planted his soles on the rug, and forced himself to stay in place, but now he kind of felt good about it, enjoyed the feeling of his soul peeling itself free from his brain.

Maybe Barry's punches had done something else to him.

You are a star.

"Are you fucking kidding me? I'm like your only fucking fan in the whole world."

You are a star…

"Why would you stop talking to the only person on this whole fucking planet that doesn't think you're a loser."

Snow crunched as his mother's car tires rolled into the driveway.

…born from the dust of an explosion…

"Because you ARE A LOSER. And your movies FUCKING SUCK. God. I tried to be nice to you and why would I when you're such a fucking asshole."

The front door opened.

…in space…

"I fucking hate you. And guess what? Your movies are absolute trash. So fucking pretentious. They don't even mean anything. They're just bullshit."

"Brock?" His mother yelled.

…and you, my friend, have been bursting ever since.

"Fuck you."

Horror is a hard genre to define, and I'm often criticized for being on the outside of it. But I write my brand of horror and I stand by it. This story is a perfect example. Most people wouldn't call this horror, but to me it's the purest horror of all, the kind we face all the time, the kind where a person lets the weight of the world change who they are. And I can't think of anything more horrific than that, because it's real, and it's happening right now, all around us, everywhere.

WINTER'S FIRST MYTH

Winter cracked his back. He thought he might die. A lack of sleep, thanks to Candlestick's hourly crying fits, a brutal day of training with Uncle Café, and an increasing demand on him to create more generators, wore down on him. He wanted a break from everything, from everyone.

Sleeping Gypsy frowned at the sight of him. "You look exhausted," she said as she bounced Candlestick on her knee.

"You would think they'd give us a break from fight training when we have a newborn." He sat next to his wife and rested his head on her shoulder. "I know I am whining to someone who also has a lot to deal with. I am sorry."

She tilted her head so her temple touched the top of his skull. "It's okay. I am stronger than you, so I don't need to whine as much."

Winter chuckled. "Where is the mischief maker?"

"I put Violin down for a nap."

Winter pried himself away from his wife and stood up. "I will check on her."

Winter walked down the hollow corridor, which was lit by a series of strip lights that only illuminated the outside edges.

The bustle of his people poured from the grow rooms, the furnace room, and the laundry area.

Winter opened the door to Violin's bedroom with a slow movement to avoid the loud creaking the door liked to give. His heart slipped from its chamber at the sight of her empty bed. He charged in, clicking on the small lamp on her nightstand, and checked the four corners of the room. She wasn't there.

He flew back into the hallway, running toward the community room. "Violin!" he shouted as he bumped into the wall. The community room was empty, everyone working in their departments. Winter tossed chairs to the side, checking under tables. His little nugget was hiding well.

As he stood up and took inventory of the room, thinking of where she could be, he noticed the door toward the forbidden tunnel was ajar. Panic washed over him, traveling through his bloodstream and pounding into his temples.

"Violin," he yelled as he pushed the door all the way open.

His heart settled as he saw his little girl walking with the wobbly gait of a four-year-old.

"Violin!"

She turned to him and smiled.

"What are you doing?" He ran to her and scooped her up, nearly crushing her with the weight of his embrace. "My dear girl. You know you're never supposed to come down this way."

She pulled her head away from him and pointed down the corridor. "Green monster."

He narrowed his eyelids. "What are you talking about?"

"Green monster," she said again and pointed.

"Show me."

Keeping her snuggled in his chest, he stepped down the corridor. He knew there would be no monsters, but worried she saw a venomous snake or something else with a bite.

When the green monster finally revealed itself, Winter laughed so loudly, his daughter jolted against his arms.

"I like him," she said.

Winter finally placed her down, letting her get close to the creature. "That, my dear, is a frog."

"Froggie. I like him."

Winter nodded, catching the excitement and questions in his daughter's eyes. "Yes, you can touch him."

She ran to it with her hands out, but he hopped away whenever she got too close. Winter didn't like how near they were all moving toward the stone slab, and he placed his hand on Violin's shoulder to stop her from going any further.

"The frog would like to leave here now, so he can get back to his home."

"Can we take him there?"

Winter shook his head. "I am afraid not. His journey is too dangerous for us. Would you like me to tell you a story about him?"

Violin smiled. "Okay."

Wheat Field tossed his hat on the bed and stretched his arms. His daughter looked up at him. "Do you have to leave, Dad?"

He rubbed his fingers on her slick green scalp. "I'm afraid I must. But I'll be back soon, and just in time for Froggelhops."

His daughter, Eggplant, danced in a circle. "Froggelhops! I hope the Frog gods bring me lots of presents."

"Now, now. A holiday is about more than getting presents."

He kissed his child before hopping off into the woods. On his journey, something caught his eye amongst a copse of trees with rustling green leaves. Behind them, something bright and colorful shook. Wheat Field hopped closer, eyeing the wonderful and vibrant thing. It was another tree, a large one with long, flat leaves, but the leaves were multicolored, iridescent like the oil used in old fashioned generators.

These leaves also rustled, but they moved in distinct patterns from the green trees in front. They weren't windblown but appeared to be shivering.

"Strange," Wheat Field said as he pulled his top hat lower on his head.

All at once, the leaves separated from their branches and twisted, twirled, and danced through the air, some floating downward, others shooting up to the sky. The colors flittered around each other, a rainbow explosion.

As they plummeted toward him, raining down hard, Wheat Field shielded himself with his forearm, covering his face.

"What's a frog doing in our wood?" a sharp, elderly female voice said.

Wheat Field removed his arm and peeked out. Standing before him was a miniature woman, no larger than him, and she had wings. Wings!

"Sorry Ma'am. I was just passing through."

"Passing through to where? And where from?"

Wheat Field cleared his throat, worried he'd introduced himself as passive, weak. "I'm from Whegothca, I'm headed to the people's world in search of goodies for my children. Froggelhops is coming."

"Froggelhops?" The woman spit the question out like a broken tooth.

Wheat Field didn't feel like explaining his people's holidays and a newfound grumpiness coursed through his blood. "Yes, it's something us frogs—"

"—I know what the holiday is, sir. I'm wondering why you are spending your time away from your family when the entire point of the holiday is to celebrate those who did the opposite. Am I not correct on that, Sir Frog? Is the holiday not a celebration of those who went out of their way to connect with their loved ones? Are frogs not exceptionally clingy in that way? While the rest of the world celebrates hard work and individuality, you green skins blather on about the honor of family connectivity."

Wheat Field narrowed his eyes. "It seems you are indeed well-versed in our ways. I have spent all year with my children and wife, and I am taking a single day to venture into the people's world for gifts for them. A surprise, you see. If I brought them, they'd know what they were getting. Besides, I worry the trek might be too dangerous for little ones."

The woman flapped her wings so fiercely it blew Wheat Field's hat off. "And dangerous it will be. You have magnificent beasts to encounter on your trip. Three of them. The Sherps, devilish horned beasts; they will tear your body to shreds. The Harzans, metal creatures who fuse to your head and melt your brain."

She paused then, staring blankly with a smile as empty as Wheat Field's top hat, which now rested lonely against a shrub. Finally, Wheat Field urged her on. "And the third?"

She tilted her head and scrunched her already wrinkly forehead. "I am the third." She turned her head to her fluttering companions. "We are the third." As she said this, she lifted her arms, and her people soared in concentric patterns around her. He stared at them in bewilderment.

"And who are you, exactly?"

"We are the fairies."

"And what will you do to me?"

She shrugged. "Protect you, of course."

Wheat Field picked up his hat, dusted it off, and pulled it onto his head. "I appreciate the offer, but I'm more of a loner. I must be going now."

He hopped forward, but the woman didn't move. A staring contest began between them. Eventually, she broke the silence. "I will send Melun and Ugly Duchess to assist you on your journey. They will fly high above and slightly behind you to keep out of your affairs. I will instruct them only to come down to help you if you run into one of the beasts."

Wheat Field licked his lips, thinking. "I suppose that will be fine, as long as they stay away."

The woman flew up and whispered to two fairies flying in spirals around each other. After she finished speaking, they nodded and flew so high in the air, Wheat Field could no longer see them.

When the old woman waved to him, Wheat Field took it as an all-clear, and hopped by the now naked tree where the fairies had once congregated. His journey took him beyond a dirt path, toward a bridge. It was a rickety old wooden thing, drooping down in the center like a frown.

He sighed and hopped from plank the plank, the bridge rocking and swaying with each bounce. When he reached the middle, a creature arose from a series of bushes at the other end. He was a big thing, covered in clumps of matted brown fur. His fangs hung so low they curled around his chin. His horns twirled upward before tangling around each other.

"Dinner. Dinner," the thing said with a voice so rattled, Wheat Field guessed the monster had stones in his throat.

Wheat Field turned only to find the side he came from now blocked by another one of the monsters.

"I'll take the legs. You can have its head," the beast said.

"Let's rip him to shreds," the other agreed.

As the two beasts closed in on him, making the bridge taut with their fierce weight, Wheat Field's mouth turned dry, and he wept at the idea of never hugging his daughter again.

He peered over the edge, wondering if he could survive the drop, but he couldn't even see the ground below. He'd splatter, for sure.

The frog gods were teaching him a lesson. A frog's duty was to stay with his loved ones, never to part unless necessary, and here Wheat Field was, diving headfirst into danger for the sake of presents. Wouldn't the gods reward his family for their dedication to each other, for never parting, for taking time for their daily duties to keep themselves company? He didn't need to get his family gifts. The gods would have rewarded them.

One beast reached his clawed fist forward, ready to squish and carve, but before his thick fingers could touch Wheat Field, a set of purple wings flew through the monster's head, sending a spray of blood to the frog's face. Wheat Field flinched as the warm liquid splashed on him. He turned to the other monster, who cried as a pink-winged fairy gouged the beast's eyes out.

"My heavens," Wheat Field said and looked back at the first beast. The purple-winged fairy dug his tiny fingers into the creature's chest cavity and pulled out gore and tendons.

"What are you doing? The thing is dead. Let him be."

The fairy looked up at Wheat Field with a face full of confusion. "They come back to life if you don't destroy them totally."

Wheat Field huffed and turned around once more. The pink fairy ripped the other monster's arms off while spitting out pieces of the thing's eyes.

Blood soaked the wooden planks on the bridge, and the howls of pain from the monsters went from echoing windstorms to struggling whispers until they were nothing more than gurgles as the mouths leaked blood like a trickling faucet.

The purple fairy put his hand on Wheat Field's shoulder. "You'll need to help us eat them. We can't finish them ourselves. We are too small."

Wheat Field wiped his brow. "I will do no such thing."

"Then the monsters will come back to life and their sole mission will be to find and kill you and everyone you have ever loved."

Wheat Field nearly fell off the bridge at the thought. A dizzy spell came over him, and his pits grew warm. "I can't."

The fairy smiled, showing his crimson-stained teeth. "You must."

Purple Wings ripped off a furry piece of leg; skin and muscle throbbed in his fist. "I am Melun. Let us enjoy dinner together."

Tears formed in Wheat Field's eyes. He had half a mind to slap Melun, but visions of these beasts killing his wife and daughter put an end to his decision-making. He gulped and took the slimy meat and furry skin from Melun's hand.

Melun's smile crawled up his purple cheeks. "To friends and feasts, we devour the beasts."

Wheat Field nodded, and his stomach lurched at the thought of this gore touching his lips.

"You're supposed to repeat it back to me," Melun said.

The pink fairy joined them, holding her own clump of gore. Her face was smeared with monster blood. "To friends and feasts, we devour the beasts," she said with a perky giddiness.

Wheat Field croaked and whispered, "To friends and feasts…"

The two fairies nodded, staring with eager anticipation.

"We devour the beasts." He shoved the clump in his mouth. A horrible taste assaulted his senses, copper and mud. As he chomped, a pool of liquid squeezed out of the meat, and it tasted like stale, grimy water. The texture matched the taste, gamey and chewy.

He finally ground it up enough to swallow it down.

Ugly Duchess licked her lips after devouring her piece. "Well, what did you think?" she asked Wheat Field.

"Horrid," he responded in a hostile tone.

It was true, of course. The meat was the worst thing he'd ever tasted, but if he told the truth, he wanted more. It was as if he'd become addicted after just a sample. His head swam, and his heart sang. "Horrid, now let's finish the job and be done with it."

The two fairies smiled at each other, and Wheat Field knew he failed to hide his anticipation.

For the next half hour, the fairies ripped meat from the Sherps, and they all took turns gnawing it down their gullets. The taste grew on Wheat Field, and the more he ate it, the more he desired it, yearned for it. Sadness and despair flooded his brain as the monsters' bodies slowly disappeared into his and the fairies' bellies, because he knew eventually he'd have nothing left to eat, and would probably never again experience the euphoria the meat provided.

When the monsters were down to nothing but bone, Wheat Field sucked on the cartilage on the ends, hoping to prolong the taste on his tongue.

"You should keep moving. The darkness approaches and more monsters will come," Ugly Duchess said.

Wheat Field dropped the bone hanging from his mouth and sighed. As soon as he walked away from the skeletons, the pure ecstasy waned, replacing itself with a deep-rooted hunger, a screwdriver-to-the-brain of a headache, and a spinning stomach.

His fairy guards flew back to their posts up in the sky, and with heavy limbs, Wheat Field carried on his journey.

After hours of hopping, the ground made way for large chunks of metal. The world itself had gone mechanical. The cliffs, trees, and earth were all made of tin, steel, copper. Wires sprouted from the ground like shrubs. Airfoils made the floor curve like mini hills. Protruding from the silvery cliffs, turbines spun, the rotors spitting wind at Wheat Field with such force, he had to walk forward at an angle. The stators stared at him like unblinking eyes.

He struggled through the wind fields. When he cleared them, he bent over and heaved for breath. Between the deep wind, the long journey, and the detoxing from monster meat, Wheat Field's body begged for a break.

But as the long, slender arms of metal trees moved, Wheat Field understood no break would come. He remembered the words of the old fairy. He'd met the Sherps. Those horned beasts he ended up feasting on. Now, a new creature moved to introduce themselves. The Harzans. The woman had warned Wheat Field that they would fuse themselves to his skull and melt his brain.

Maybe this would scare him less if he had his strength, but with each muscle in his frog body aching, he wouldn't even have the heart to run away.

His fairy guardians kept him from screaming in terror. He'd seen what they were capable of, and since they'd protected him so well from the Sherps, he steeled himself with the knowledge they'd soon come down to rescue him yet again.

But the Harzan monsters, three of them, surrounded Wheat Field and moved dangerously close for his liking.

"Ugly Duchess? Melun? Are you coming?"

One of the Harzans wrapped its silvery tentacle fingers around Wheat Field's neck, and tiny worm-like wires escaped through the gaps where the metal pieces hadn't fused together. These wires danced upward like candle smoke, coming toward Wheat Field's temples.

He belched a holler. "Help me!" Looking all over the sky, Wheat Field saw no signs of his protectors.

As his pulse throbbed, blood gushing toward his heart, his mind traveled to peaceful memories of home. He and his wife sitting in their rocking chairs, sewing clothes for their daughter, passionately in love, and speaking whispers of adoration with nothing more than the occasional eye contact. He and his daughter playing hide and seek. His wife and Eggplant coming with him to work in the kitchen, unwilling to separate from him.

And then his memories turned to the ominous signs he should not have ignored. His wife telling him to stay, that no gift was worth his absence. Eggplant begging him not to leave. The dreams of the frog gods leering down at him for putting adventure before family.

As the cold, slithery wires touched his temples, his mind returned to the present. He could not allow his family to live the rest of their lives with only the shadows of a memory. They needed him, and he, them.

A rage built in his chest, an electric current that charged his inner strength and determination.

His tongue lashed from his mouth and slapped against one of the Harzan's foreheads, knocking the machine to the ground. Wheat Field's forearm cracked into the torso of another beast, sending the thing on top of its friend. With one last standing machine, Wheat Field leaped and kicked it in the chest.

He hopped on top of its flailing body and punched its face over and over.

As he gripped a button eye and planned to rip it from the thing's head, the fairies finally arrived. They fluttered over his shoulders, watching his violence with eager anticipation.

"Destroy it. Its insides are as tasty as the Sherp's," Ugly Duchess whispered.

Wheat Field's eyes narrowed, and he gasped. He released his fingers from the machine and stood staring at his surroundings. The metal things stared at him, fear in their eyes. The fairies beamed with delight.

"Kill them all," Melun said.

"I understand now," Wheat Field murmured, and hopped away from what was almost a scene of carnage.

"What do you understand?" Melun asked.

Wheat Field put his head down. "The fairy woman who leads you told me there were three creatures. The Sherps, who destroy the body. The Harzan, who destroy the mind. Then there is you. She didn't say this, but I now understand you destroy the soul."

He hopped away from the metal things. "You can chase me if you'd like, but I won't fight you. I'll allow you to destroy yourselves in the chase, though. And I will win."

The metal things stood up, staring blankly, not understanding. But they didn't chase him either. Meanwhile, the fairies followed behind, continuing their assault on his spirit.

"Don't you want to feed?"

"Didn't you enjoy the taste?"

"Won't you desire the feeling again?"

He fought them by ignoring them, and the pain in his muscles, the agonizing want in his blood, the throbbing and yearning in his brain. He defeated them by reminding himself who he was, who his family loved, who they expected to return. They were relentless for a long time, but eventually understood his spirit was made of a thicker steel than the Harzans.

And when he was finally alone, he hopped into a tunnel where a magical community lived. One with food, and trinkets, and delights galore, and he knew those in this community wouldn't hurt him for his intrusion, because they, too, had steel spirits and a love for family.

Violin's chest moved in and out against Winter's torso as he carried her back toward her room. She'd fallen asleep in the first few minutes of his story, but he finished it anyway. He'd need the practice, because he dreamed of a life with many tales, a familial bonding with words and imagination.

He supposed he told the story as much for himself as his daughter.

The frog, too, had long since abandoned his tale, escaping the tunnel into the outside world where Winter himself would never dare go.

He closed the door to the tunnel and stood in the small room that connected it to the community room. Something about this small, square little place always gave him the shivers, as if it were filled with evil and horror.

His back arched and a creeping ivy of tingles slithered up his spine as he moved out of the dark space. As he shut the second door, blocking out the cold and violent world beyond, he heard something. His brow furrowed, and he placed his ear to the door. Fluttering. Wings. And a horrific giggle.

Since Winter's Myths Season 2 released, the most common question I get asked is when Season 3 will arrive. My fans even jokingly call me George R. R. Martin because they've been waiting so long. I always respond that Season 3 has come out already. It's called Bunker Dogs. And Season 4 is called On a Clear Day, You Can See Block Island. This, of course, is a joke, because there will be a Winter's Myths Season 3, but the joke isn't without some truth. Winter's Myths does and will continue to encapsulate the entire world of DreadPop that I've created, and those stories ARE all part of the Winter's Myths legacy. It will all tie together in what I hope will be shocking stories. My newest serial story, The Block Island Dead, hints at all those tethers as well. This story is for the fans of Winter's Myths, and probably won't matter much to those who didn't get into the series. Within it, there are A LOT of hints toward future secrets.

LEVITATING

Dylan slowly spun his glass, watching the condensation run down the rim to the epoxied wood bar top. A lovely ringlet formed around the glass. Little bubbles slid up the side and joined a dancing orgy underneath the foamy head.

In the same way smelling pine brought him back to childhood Christmases, the sights, sounds, and smells of Amber's Tavern transported Dylan to a million past lives, all of them regretful, yet all of them tinted with rosy joyous memories tonight. Greasy fried food sizzled in the back, and the smell of chicken and onion rings wafted through the kitchen's double doors. Music from the digital jukebox thumped through the shitty speakers on the opposite side of the bar, where a group of women in their late thirties laughed and screeched like first-time drinkers. They sat at two tables shoved together to accommodate their group size. Neon green and orange lights ran across the ceiling's molding.

A couple sat across from Dylan, where the bar wrapped around, and whenever the screeching women yelled and Dylan looked up to see the commotion, the couple stared at him as if he were offending them by glancing in their direction. A few other folks sat on bar stools playing Keno, most of them regulars that Dylan recognized from ten years prior. He wasn't surprised they hadn't changed but was slightly surprised they were still alive and rolling.

The bartenders were new though. Both young women, attractive, full of smiles and jokes. They'd probably make a killing somewhere else where people outside the local drunks went. The folks in here were counting quarters to pay their bar tab half the time, and Dylan knew this because he used to be one of them. Just down the road, Fitzpatrick's filled the seats with lightweight college kids spilling in from Providence and North Kingstown who spent Mom and Dad's money buying expensive shots and liquor they couldn't handle.

Dylan wrapped his hand around the glass but hesitated to lift it. He wasn't debating it. He'd long passed that point. He knew he'd drink the beer, and then another and another. He nearly drooled at the prospect. He just wasn't sure when. He needed something profound to happen, something special to mark the occasion.

The jukebox switched from "I'm Too Sexy" by Right Said Fred to "Africa" by Toto. The women apparently loved that, because they hooted and hollered as the song began. Dylan shot them a glance. While all of the women laughed and cheered, some of them vocalizing the guitar riff, one woman sat staring at Dylan, unblinking. It gave him a shiver. He turned and looked behind him to see if someone or something else had caught her eye and it just appeared as if she were staring at him, but nothing was there other than a wall and a few empty tables.

He risked another look, and still, she stared. She wasn't hiding it, not looking away when he caught her eye. She just watched him. There was no anger in her eyes, no excitement. It was like she was studying him.

She won the staring contest. He put his head down,

returning his attention to his beer. His fingers slid against the wet surface.

He felt her eyes still burning into him, and it made him uncomfortable. One more look. She was still staring, and this time, as soon as he looked at her, she leaned back and crossed her arms, a smile working up one side of her face.

If he weren't so uncomfortable, he would have looked at her for other reasons. She was gorgeous. Red hair flowed over her shoulders. She wore bright red lipstick, but otherwise dressed fairly dark in opposition of her pale skin. Her dress was black and gothic, sheer mesh in places and lace trimmed. With the table in the way, he couldn't tell how that played out with most of her body, but on the upper half, it revealed her black bra and a lot of her skin.

Her friends were all dressed colorfully, like women in their thirties having a night out after a long work week, but the staring woman looked more like she wore something outrageous for the sake of it. He didn't mean that to mock the dress or the style, but she wore it like a Halloween costume, not as someone who normally dressed that way.

The couple across the bar stopped caring if he was staring at them and had since moved toward rubbing up on each other. They held hands above the bar and were snaking their fingers around each other's. He presumed they'd be gone soon, rushing home to finish off their date in what would surely be a disappointing sexual experience for both of them. Fuck. He hadn't even had a sip yet and the negativity had already wormed its way back into his head. But seriously, who molests their significant other's hands like that unless they were on ecstasy or really, really out of practice?

He snapped out of it. The patrons of the bar were distracting him. It didn't fall short on him that he probably used them for that purpose intentionally. His heart raced as he returned his focus to the beer. "Africa" ended and "Hit Me Baby One More Time" came on. The women at the table shouted. One of them stood up and started dancing around the empty tables nearby. The rest of her group followed suit and spilled onto the makeshift dance floor. All of them except Staring Girl, who remained lasered in on Dylan with her arms crossed.

Maybe she was the profound thing he needed for the moment he took his first swallow, that glaring anomaly to mark the moment in time when he fell. He grabbed the glass and brought it to his lips. The sip went down smoothly, and it instantly brought warmth to his chest. He felt his shoulders relax. God, he'd missed it.

The first sip led to the second and the third. He eyed the dancing women with a newfound lack of giving a fuck, and then slid his sight toward the staring woman. As soon as their eyes locked, she shook her head, sat forward, and grabbed a glass of pink liquid from her table. She downed it in one go.

Dylan furrowed his brow. What was that about?

She placed the glass back down and finally looked away from him. Dylan took a deep breath, feeling freer. She hopped out of her seat and joined the dancing party, all smiles and laughter.

With that over, he finished the rest of his drink and ordered another. One was all he needed for the lightheaded-ness and all-around good buzz to flow through him. If he could hold down that feeling, he'd grab it and ride it until death do them part, but he planned to keep guzzling until he felt like shit instead.

With his second beer in hand, he slid through his Face-book feed, looking at or for nothing in particular. Just trying to waste time. The couple across from him left, and one of the regulars at the Keno station, too. But some new people came in. Young, loud kids. About twenty of them. Dylan had come to Amber's solely to avoid that type of crowd, so he decided he'd have one more, and then pick up a case at the liquor store before they closed. He'd finish getting obliterated in the peace of his own living room.

The women kept dancing, but they quieted down when the kids showed up, looking a bit nervous to catch their attention. College-age boys can be obnoxious toward women, if not dangerous, and these women seemed well aware of that.

Dylan went back to his phone. The college kids were all shouting at each other. With boys that age, Dylan could never tell if they were having fun or fighting with one another. Either way, they were loud and stupid.

Someone sat next to him, but he refused to look up. College kids often came looking to get into a fight with anyone they could, so if one of them encroached on his space, they probably wanted a reaction from him.

"Long way down, huh?" a silky voice said.

He looked up to see the staring woman smiling at him. "Huh?"

Her smile stretched further up her cheeks, and she reached out a delicate hand. Her nails were painted black. "I'm Victoria."

Something about her being so close to him gave him chills as if her body spit out electricity and shocked his flesh. He gave his hand to hers, and they shook, and that, too, made his skin prickle. "Dylan."

She laughed. "I know. Wow. Am I *that* forgettable?"

Shit. He knew her from somewhere. That explained the staring. Well, kind of. It made it slightly less weird, anyway. He didn't hide his unknowing, tilting his head and squinting at her. "I'm sorry. I know this is going to sound like a cheesy pickup line, but I can't imagine I would forget you if I knew you."

"I'm usually in a hoodie and sweatpants when you see me." She spun in her stool and waved to the bartender. When the server came over, Victoria said, "Can I get a vodka and watermelon, and my friend here will have a…"

It took Dylan way too long to realize she paused for his sake. "Oh. Ah, I'll have a Pumpkinhead."

The bartender left to make their drinks. Victoria put her hand on Dylan's. "I would not have guessed a Pumpkinhead in a million years."

Moving his hand away from her touch, he chuckled. "It was Blue Moon earlier. But I like when they put the cinnamon on the rim for the Pumpkinheads. It's good to switch it up once in a while."

She placed an elbow on the counter, and rested her chin in her hand, never taking her eyes off him. It was uncanny how she could unabashedly glare at someone like that. "You're an interesting character Dylan."

Dylan downed the last drips of his retired glass and slid it away. "Remind me again how I know you."

"No."

"I'm sorry?"

"No. You don't get off that easy. You have to figure it out."

The bartender returned with their drinks. Victoria held her glass up. "To spiraling."

Without putting any thought into her words, he clinked glasses with her and took a big swig. Then it clicked. He put his drink down, sadness stealing the moment from him. "I figured it out."

She sunk a little, too. "Yeah."

"You weren't at all of them, though. Just Mondays, right?"

She spun three-sixty in her seat, like a child. "Baptist on 91."

Dylan thought of his friends there, and wondered what they'd say if they saw him right now. "Baptist on 91. One of the more boring ones."

She laughed. "Painfully."

"So, how long?"

"How long was I sober or how long have I been back at it?"

He shrugged. "Both, I guess."

"Four years and about…" She looked at the clock on the wall. "Half an hour."

"Fuck." A stone dropped from Dylan's throat to his guts.

"Truth is, I didn't plan on drinking tonight. Some work friends invited me out, and I was just gonna stick to drinking non-alcoholics—side note, they don't know I'm sober, so let's keep that between us. Well, I guess I'm not sober anymore, oops—but then I saw the great Dylan Huddle sitting at the bar with a glass in front of him. Might have assumed you were having a non-alcoholic, too, if not for the pained look on your face."

He rubbed his eyes. "So, it's my fault you drank?"

She rolled her eyes. "You've had what? Ten years of meetings, and you think I broke sobriety just because you did? I'm an alcoholic. I was looking for an excuse."

He took another swig. He'd long passed the tipsy phase, traipsing around in full-on drunk mode. "Sounds like the same thing to me. Still feels like my fault."

She leaned in and he saw something briefly. Her eyes changed to red, and not the kind of red you see in photos when the lighting is bad, but a deep, burning red. It disappeared in a flash, and her eyes turned back to the light blue of a tropical ocean. Both were equally as hypnotizing.

He blinked it away and chalked it up to his drunkenness.

"It feels like your fault because you have the ego of an alcoholic. You're not getting it. I wanted to get drunk. I used you as an excuse. If you weren't here, something else would have been my reason. If you didn't drop the bomb, the explosion ain't your fault, even if you inspired the war."

The asshole kids were shouting again, and Dylan's internal alarms went off, telling him trouble brewed and he should get the fuck out before those douchebags beat the ever-loving shit out of him for no reason other than to release their pent-up testosterone.

"I think I should get going. It was nice to meet you, and I'm sorry we never chatted at any of the meetings. But I'll look for you next week because, hopefully, we'll both be there."

"Come on, don't leave yet. I want to chat a little more. I think we both know neither of us will be there Monday."

He shivered. It was true, although he hadn't fully convinced himself of it yet. He wanted to believe he was a sober person pretending to be a drunk for one night, and not a drunk person pretending to be sober for a decade.

One of the drunk college kids yelled something and punched a wall. The volatile action sent an unsettling quiet throughout the bar. The two bartenders looked too scared to tell them off, and the regulars had years of practice slinking away from bullshit. Victoria's work friends were sipping the dregs of their glasses through straws, looking to hurry up and leave. Dylan was glad for the wall punch. It gave him all the flow he needed to get the fuck out, despite how much Victoria worked him with her vibe. "Sorry, but that's my cue."

"What, them?" Victoria took a sip from her glass, letting an ice cube slip into her mouth. She crushed it with her teeth and said with a mouth full of ice chips, "Gimme one second."

Dylan turned his stool straight, keeping his eyes on his drink, but using the position to watch what Victoria did through his peripheral. She approached the group. Dylan tensed, but everyone remained silent. He shot a look over there and saw Victoria whispering to one of the guys. The rest of his friends watched with the same curiosity Dylan did.

She spun around on her heels. Her black dress twirled with her, and Dylan noticed for the first time that it was adorned with black ribbon and dark red roses. It looked like a Tim Burton prop, and wholly out of place on her. She came back over and sat next to him. "See, no problem."

"What do you mean?"

Behind him, the crowd of college kids argued about something, but not in the hostile way they had before. Lots of, "Aw, come on," and "Seriously?"

A few seconds later, the boy Victoria had whispered to appeared at the stool on Dylan's other side.

"I'd like to cash out," he said.

"See," Victoria added. "He's cashing out. They're leaving."

Dylan leaned in, not wanting the kid to hear, afraid to be associated with whatever had happened. "What did you say to him?"

She ran her finger along the rim of her glass and said in a sultry voice, "I'm very persuasive." Then she broke into a giggle. "Sorry, that was my attempt at Morticia Addams. It was bad, I know."

"Let me get their drinks, too," the kid said as he handed his card to the bartender. "Is there a way to add like another hundred for whatever they drink after this?"

Victoria sat up, looking over Dylan. "We'll both have two more drinks before we leave, so you can just add those in now. We don't need more than that. I'll just keep on with the vodka and watermelon, and Dylan will have…"

He understood the assignment this time, but two more drinks felt like more than he could handle. He was already very drunk. Still, he kind of wanted this conversation to play out, and since Victoria the Magician flashed her wand and turned his bill to dust, it made the decision a bit easier. "I'll go back to Blue Moons."

The kid and the bartender squared away, and the group of college dicks left. Victoria's coworkers came by and told her they were leaving, too.

"I'm not, though. I'm going to stay here with Dylan."

One of her friends clutched Victoria's shoulder. "I don't know if that's a good idea. You always leave the bar with who you arrived with."

Victoria pried the woman's hand away. "Good philosophy

in general, but I promise I'm fine. Dylan and I are old friends, and we have lots of catching up to do."

He almost shot out of his seat and yelled, "THERE IT IS!" because he saw that red flash in her eyes again. But no one else did. Her coworkers had been looking right at her, and no one else said, "Hey, why the fuck do your eyes do that?"

"But you drove with us."

"I'll call an Uber."

Victoria and her friends debated a little longer before she convinced them to leave her alone, which she only did by promising to text them when she left the bar and again when she arrived home. Dylan respected that she had friends looking out for her, but Victoria seemed wildly annoyed by it.

Their bartender brought them their penultimate round before disappearing into the back room with the other bartender and the kitchen staff. Dylan and Victoria sat alone in the bar, everyone else gone. Even the Keno playing regulars.

Victoria sipped her drink. "So, what brought you here?"

He pretended this was all normal, that he wasn't delving into insanity personified. "Oh, this is where I used to drink most nights. I had a buddy who worked second shift at the mill, and he'd pick me up. We'd come here and drink ourselves rotten. Of course, I was always drunk before he picked me up. I worked from home, so I could do that. I used to wake up drinking and fall asleep on the couch with a bottle in my hand."

"I meant what brought you to drink again. Wife left you? Lost your job? I think most people break sobriety just because of temptation. But you look like you planned this out. I don't mean to be a bitch, but it was like watching a suicide."

Dylan wiped foam from his upper lip. "No wife. I broke up with my last girlfriend about three months ago, and while I haven't really dated since, I'm not feeling desperately lonely or anything like that. Didn't lose my job, and I work for myself, so I don't hate my boss. Well, I guess I do sometimes, but that's not why I'm here either."

She turned her stool a few degrees, and her knee touched his. "I notice you didn't refute the suicide comment, but, moving on. So, if not a relationship or job, what brought you down? I have to admit, of all the folks who spoke at those meetings, you sounded the most resolute."

Dylan sipped. He needed the time to think of his answer because, in truth, he wasn't sure himself. When he put the glass down, now half-full, he turned to her with liquid confidence. He let his full leg touch against hers, his knee bunching her dress. "I guess I couldn't bear to do another day as me. As the me who existed a few hours ago."

She accepted his closeness and let him know it by putting her hand on his upper thigh. "So, you think drunk you will be a better you?"

He laughed and matched her by putting his hand on her upper thigh, although he had a lot more clothing between his hand and her skin thanks to the bunching of the dress. "No. Not a better me. A different me."

"A worse you?" Her pointer and middle finger rubbed gently against his jeans. Electricity.

"Yes." He moved his hand down to the bottom of her dress, just below her knee.

"You'd choose a worse you just to have a different you?"

His heart pounded and for the first time in a long time, he liked the feeling. "Yes. I just want some damned chaos."

She leaned closer and whispered in his ear. "I want to fuck you."

Chaos.

Every alarm bell went off. He'd had dozens of one-night stands in his life, but this one felt wrong. It was a trick, some kind of sleight of hand by the machinations of life. He was being played by evil forces, and he meant that most literally. Victoria wasn't a normal person. She was beautiful and had that manic-pixie bullshit attitude you only see in movies, and her eyes flashed red. Dylan sat with a fucking ghost, like the punchline in a kid's horror story. *And then she lured him out onto the very road she died on 50 years earlier.*

Jesus. Her fingertips sent waves of electricity into his flesh. What would her tongue do?

He leaned in and kissed her to find out. Dylan had hoped the drink would kill him, but maybe the devil was better.

She opened her mouth and accepted his tongue, but she didn't react much otherwise. His tongue did all the work, and he felt let down, expecting her to devour him. He thought a bolt would course through his bloodstream and explode his heart, but instead, it felt like a kiss. A half-hearted one at that.

When they separated, she grabbed her drink and finished it. "We still have one more."

He furrowed his brow. "I'm willing to skip it."

"Be patient." She waved to the bartender who leaned against the kitchen door, head resting by the oval window.

The bartender popped the door open. "Ready for your last round?"

Dylan really wanted to refuse his last drink, worried about how sloppy he was getting, and afraid he'd fall asleep or do something else stupid to ruin his chance with Victoria. He'd never wanted something more than he wanted her right now, and he didn't want to fumble it. Or maybe he did, because she also terrified him. She was a tidal wave shrouding him in her shadow. He knew she'd drown him, but he couldn't help but stare in awe as she came crashing down on him.

He also worried the kiss had ruined something. They weren't touching anymore, each facing forward, and not even really looking at each other. The electricity escaped.

When their drinks arrived, Victoria rested her head in her hand again and mixed hers with her fingertip before licking it clean. "I want more from your story."

"What story?"

"Why you brought yourself back to the drink tonight."

"I want to know *your* story." Fuck. Were his words slurring?

She shrugged and sipped her drink. "Ask away."

"Where dayawork?" Yup, his words were slurring.

"Third-grade teacher."

He laughed. "Yeah, right."

"No one ever believes me. Those women here tonight were all teachers at Tanner's Switch Elementary. Look it up on Google right now. One of the first pictures will be from the Westerly Sun, and it'll show all of us smiling for the camera when we had our big science day."

He put his hands up. "Okay. Okay. I believe you. So, why are you drinking?"

She spun again, bringing back the closeness, their knees reaching each other with a satisfying twick of electricity. Coincidentally, as that jolt shot up Dylan's spine, the lighting in the bar flickered. Not dramatically, but enough that Dylan noticed it.

"I already told you. Because you are."

"But you said you were just looking for an excuse. Why?"

She clasped her hands over his. He heard a crackling sound, like a lit sparkler, as their skin met. Maybe one of the college kids slipped acid into his drink. It wasn't just the red eyes and weird electric thing, but his overall paranoid state. He truly feared her, but also couldn't stop himself from progressing to wherever she led them. He craved her, wanted to tear her clothes off and bend her over the bar. But he was terrified and wanted to run to his car. Was it his fight-or-flight that caused his rapid breathing, or his excitement?

She said, "I don't know. I just feel like I'm racing all the time, charging toward..." she trailed off.

"Toward what?"

"Toward *the* end. You know what I mean?"

Dylan sat up straight. "You feel like you're walking closer

and closer to death and spending it all just trying to avoid—"
he scrunched his face, trying to find the word "—difficulties?"

Her eyes flashed red again. Dylan bit back the groan that
almost escaped his throat as panic bubbled in his guts.

Victoria grabbed her drink, swirled it, stared at it, then
gulped it down in a single swallow. She breathed a sigh of
relief and closed her eyes as if the alcohol were transporting
her to a dream world. "It's not quite that. Sometimes, I don't
feel alive at all. I wake up. I teach kids. I go home and plan my
next day. Not just the work, but my meals, my bedtime. I
count my calories. I treat my body right. And sometimes I
want to slam my head into a dead end."

Dylan snapped his fingers. "That's it. That's exactly it. I
wanted to slam my head into a dead end. I love that."

She laughed and licked her lips. "Finish your drink, then,
and we'll go slam our heads into the wall together."

"I don't think I should. I mean with the drink, not the
other part. It's just, I'm already sloppy."

She shook her head and her voice turned sharp, dictator-
ial. "You're fine. Finish it."

A weakness came over him, like all of his muscles wanted
to quit at the same time until his body spilled off his seat onto
the hard floor below. He did not want the drink. But she told
him to have it, and he would obey. That scared the shit out of
him. He brought the glass to his lips and downed the rest of it.

"Let's go," he said.

They held hands as they dipped out the side door. As they
moved around the building toward the back parking lot,
Dylan bumped into the wall. He was beyond drunk, and knew
he had no chance of performing well.

When he bumped into the wall a second time, Victoria
laughed and pushed him until his back pressed hard into the
uneven brick. They kissed with him pinned there, and she
slowly moved her hand from his chest to between his legs.
This was the kiss he'd envisioned the first time. Jolts of elec-

tricity drove down his throat, meeting his heart with bursts of energy.

The button on his jeans came undone, and her hand slid underneath his boxers until she was stroking his dick. Blood rushed to his head. He felt dizzy. Her touch was killing him. Victoria's lips slipped away from his and moved to his neck. She licked it gently as she continued to move her hand up and down his shaft.

As drunk as he was, he thought he might cum already. Usually, he struggled to keep it up when he drank. But not tonight. Victoria was heaven. She was hell. Just as he almost exploded, she took her hand off him and moved it slowly to his pants pocket. She reached in and took out his car keys, whispering in his ear, "I'll drive. You're too drunk." And with that, she walked into the lot.

Fighting vertigo, he quickly buttoned his pants shut and ran to catch up to her, just now realizing something. "How aren't you? You matched me drink for drink, and your drinks were harder than mine. How are you keeping it together?"

She clicked the unlock button on the key fob, and Dylan's Subaru Outback chirped. "There she is," Victoria said.

Dylan stumbled as he approached the car, and Victoria caught him, wrapping one arm under his and around his back. He leaned into her. "I can't believe I'm this drunk."

Victoria opened the passenger door. "In ya go," she said.

He obeyed. Why did he keep doing that? He was letting a stranger take his keys and drive his car. Victoria waltzed around the front, and he watched her. Even her walk sex appeal. She hopped in. "Your place or mine?" she asked.

"Uh, I guess it doesn't matter to me. My apartment is shit. So, probably yours."

She frowned and considered it. "Nah, we're banging our heads into walls. If your apartment is shit, let's go there."

He gasped, "I might be too drunk for this."

She turned to him. "Look at me."

He faced her, but his eyes glanced all around. It hurt to stare at her full-on.

"At me," she said.

He obeyed.

She licked her thumb and placed it on his forehead, then she leaned in and whispered, "Close your eyes."

He did. Her thumb pressed harder into the space between his eyes. "You're sobering up. Not completely sober. That wouldn't be fun. But the alcohol is slipping from your system. You're in that perfect fun zone where you're feeling the effects without going overboard."

Her thumb left his forehead, creating a cold spot from its absence. He wanted it back, for her to keep it there forever.

"Okay, you can open your eyes now."

He did. She twiddled her fingers around the ignition button, not pressing it, but getting close.

"I don't think your magic worked," Dylan said, but it had. Even his speech had improved. That was insane, of course. If his speech improved, it was no different from a placebo.

"What do you like to listen to while you drive? Is your phone connected to the Apple CarPlay? I'm so excited to hit this button and see what happens when the car comes to life. Will I get Backstreet Boys, or true crime podcasts, or audiobooks, or what? I have no idea. Are you ready to find out?"

She hit the button. The air conditioning fired a warm burst of air. "Oof, hope that cools down quickly." It took a few seconds for the Bluetooth to connect, and Dylan wondered as much as Victoria what would pour from the speakers. He couldn't remember what he had listened to on the way in.

The opening to "Street Spirit" by Radiohead came on. "Oh God, dude. You really did want to come here hating life, huh? Honestly, I expected the Encanto soundtrack."

He said nothing, just stared at her, awed. What the hell was he dealing with here? He swam in the smokey plumes of the dragon's exhalations and waited for her to encapsulate him in flame. Burn him to the ground. Part of him wished she'd just get it done with already. End it. But more than with anything in recent memory, he wanted more. To know more. To experience more. To entangle more.

"I feel weird," Dylan said.

He couldn't think. Trapped within the confines of the Outback, he convinced himself fully that she was a ghost, and she messed with his head. He couldn't say no to her. Couldn't run away. And now that he thought about it, he truly wasn't drunk anymore. A little tipsy, maybe, but not falling over drunk like he'd been. Had her little fucked up magic trick worked? No one could sober up so fast. She also pulled a magic trick on the college kids. She really was a witch, or some kind of spirit.

"Where do I go?" she asked

"Go left onto Park Ave and stay on it until you get to the Stop and Shop."

She smiled and turned right out of the parking lot. "Just gotta make a stop somewhere first."

A minute later, she pulled into a gas station parking lot.

"What are we doing here?"

"Snacks," she said and jumped out of the car. She had so much energy, beaming and radiant. She could swallow him whole, and he'd thank her for it.

He leaned his head back and closed his eyes, suddenly desperate for sleep, the kind that only drunkenness could deliver, where he'd pass out and fall deeply into a dark abyss unlike any the earth could provide otherwise.

She returned in no time, or maybe it had been a lot of time. Dylan might have drifted off. She tossed a paper bag into the backseat. "Okay, now I need the directions to your house."

They drove in silence, only breaking it when Dylan told her where to turn. "Street Spirit" turned into "Better Man" by Pearl Jam. Victoria refrained from any mocking comments.

Then, she turned the music down and said in a soft tone, "I lied to you about something."

"What?"

"I'm not a third-grade teacher."

"I kind of figured." But he hadn't. If she wasn't a teacher, she was a damned good liar, because she had way too many details to back it up. The newspaper doing a story on their science fair? And then she unspooled that thread with stories about her life as a teacher and how it led her to drink tonight. Was this woman all smoke and mirrors, tricks of light and illusion?

"I went back to school in my thirties, and that's when my addiction took a turn for the worse. It had been there a long time, but it wasn't until I was back at college that it got out of control. I was working part-time as a cashier at CVS. Still living with my mom. And going back to school full-time. Even though I was, like, trying to do something to better my life, I felt like shit all the time. How did I get to my thirties with nothing to show for it? And all day, I sat with kids who had their whole lives ahead of them and they didn't give a shit about their classes, and I was the weird older lady sitting next to them, wanting to drink and party as much as they did, wanting to have sex and be wild still.

"Then I went to work with kids doing the same job I was. I never even tried to be a manager or anything. Anyway, it was easy to drink and pop pills and snort coke while I went to school and worked. My classes weren't hard. Cashiering sure as fuck wasn't hard, outside of dealing with the most entitled assholes all day. I used to pour vodka into 20 ounces of Pepsi, and I'd stock my car with them. Jesus, I was always smashed, and I always drove. Fuck, I'm doing that now, aren't I?" She chuckled, but there was shame in it.

"Anyway, I graduated, barely, with a nursing degree, and I knew I had to sober up. It was getting out of control. I wasn't eating, or when I did, it was like soup or something that my stomach could hold down. I woke up with a glass of vodka. If I didn't take pills throughout the day, I would shake and feel sick. So, I sobered up, detoxed, did the whole deal, and went to the meetings. Shortly after, I started working at Rhode Island Hospital. And every Monday, I saw you."

Dylan looked at her as she stared at the road ahead. Her eyes were celestial blue. Putting aside all of the oddities of the night, he could consider himself a lucky man to be sitting next to such a beautiful woman. He pictured her in the hoodie and sweatpants that she wore to meetings. She didn't speak, he remembered. Never. And the Monday meetings were packed, so he'd never gotten a good look at her, or really paid much attention, but now he wished he could. He would love to see her face tucked under a hood, hiding from the world. And he wished he could extend a hand and say, "I'm Dylan. We'll be okay." But he hadn't done those things, and now they weren't okay.

"So, you're a nurse," he said. "Why hide it?"

"Was. I just wanted to play someone different tonight. Someone a little eccentric and with a weird backstory that wasn't my own. I mean, look at this fucking dress."

"Ah. I see. Do you want to talk about that *was?*"

She didn't respond for a few minutes, and Dylan took that to mean she did not want to discuss it, but then she squeaked, and he realized she was crying. She said, "I did an override and grabbed the wrong medication. The patient was a kid. She almost died. I did everything right after that, reported it immediately, filled out the paperwork. Normally, it would have been okay. Psychologically, I would have been fucked up for life, but in terms of my job, it shouldn't have gone the way it did. But the patient happened to be Governor Lawrence's daughter, and he went on a kick about hospitals and under-staffing and long hours. He never blamed me, but he blamed the environment."

Dylan leaned his head back, completely absorbed in her

world. For the first time, he met the real her, not the character in the goth dress. The ghost was human, or at least had been. "Which meant the hospital needed to put the blame firmly in your hands before the microscope hovered above their roof."

She nodded. "Basically, yeah. They were quick to point out I was only two hours into my shift, but what they failed to point out was that I worked twelve hours the night before and came back in eight hours later. Anyway, the writing was on the wall. They were pushing for dismissal. They hinted I should quit, and I was angry enough to accept that idea."

"Turn left at the next street," Dylan said.

She clicked the blinker. "And now I feel just like I did in college. I'm in my late thirties, and I have nothing to show for it. I'll probably move back in with my mother."

"And that's why you drank tonight?"

"No." She turned the wheel onto Dylan's road.

"I live in the mill building coming up on the right."

She pulled into the parking lot, examining the towering mill building. Dylan felt self-conscious, as if she were checking him out and not the building he lived in.

She parked the car and grabbed the bag in the back seat. "Ready? Lead the way."

She followed him into the building and onto the elevator. As it brought them up, Dylan said, "So, it wasn't the job that brought you to drink?"

She looked at him with the same focused stare she gave him at the bar. "I had no interest in drinking or doing drugs again. I went to the meeting last Monday, and you talked. You told everyone about hitting those lows and knowing you just have to take it one day at a time, and I thought, 'This guy is my rock.' I didn't even know you, but you spoke to me. Then the nurses I worked with were so pissed about what happened and they wanted to take me out, and I was fine with it because I've pretended to drink at the bars before. Non-alcoholic girlie drinks and alcoholic ones all look the same. And when I saw you there, it wasn't like, 'Oh no, Dylan is drinking,' it was like, 'How wild is it that the night I've put myself in a position where I could weaken happens to be the night the guy I considered my rock is also sitting in a fucking bar.' So, it wasn't you, Dylan. It was the kismet nature of you."

Dylan squinted, unwilling to take the pass she offered. "Sooooooooooo, it was because of me?"

"Not yet," she said. The elevator dinged and the door opened. She stepped away from the threshold. "I'm following you," she said, and he wasn't sure if she meant for him to lead her to his apartment or if she was answering his question. And what the hell did *not yet* mean?

As they walked the long hallway to his apartment, he grew increasingly nervous about her seeing it. It was a mess. He had a bedroom, but he'd recently put his mattress on the floor of his living room so he could fall asleep watching Netflix movies. He left half-empty water bottles all over the floor, maybe even a few crumb-filled plates. It looked like a college kid's place.

His heart raced as he opened the door. She said nothing, just walked in like she'd been there a million times. Stepping over the corner of the mattress, she dropped her paper bag on the kitchen island. She reached in and took out two small bottles of vodka.

"You got those at the gas station?"

"And these," she reached in and pulled out a baggie of pills. Dylan could tell from a single glance they weren't all the same kind. There were probably about 20 in the bag, far more than two freshly off-the-wagon people could handle in a single night, and who knows what they cost her. He hadn't taken pills in years, so he knew nothing about the street value.

"Jesus."

"My old dealer works at that gas station. Dude sells everything from liquor to coke, and he sells it from right behind that register. How he hasn't been caught or robbed or murdered is beyond me."

She tossed one of the vodka bottles to Dylan and twisted the cap off hers. He caught it and followed her lead.

"Let's get wrecked," she said and knocked down a swig.

He kept his bottle at his side and watched her, the way she closed her eyes, and how the tension visibly left her shoulders. He recognized it and yearned for it. Then it all clicked, how she'd been able to tolerate so much drinking, how she never appeared sloppy. She'd mentioned not letting her coworkers know she was sober. "Let me guess, you told the bartender when you got there tonight to give you the same non-alcoholic drink no matter what you pretended to order."

She reached into the baggie and took two pills out. They danced in her palm as she shook her hand, staring at them like long-lost friends. "Bingo," she said and dropped the pills into her mouth. With a gulp of the vodka, they were gone.

"I'm watching you break right now in real time, aren't I?"

She licked her teeth, and her eyes flashed red again. "I think you owe me that."

He stepped toward her and placed his vodka on the island, no longer thirsting for its contents, and certainly unconcerned about her eyes. "What if I don't want to watch you break?"

She stood up, took another sip, placed the bottle down, and wrapped her arms around his neck. "You think I enjoyed seeing you do it?"

"You should stop now," he said.

She put a finger over his mouth. "You should stop now." She pushed off him, and grabbed two more pills, placing them on the island's smooth faux-marble top. "Drink," she said as she danced around the island, headed for the drawers by the sink.

"What are you doing?"

She spun to him in a cutesy twirl. "I said drink, my friend. Or don't. But please don't lecture." And she went back to the drawers, opening one, then closing it, until she got to the silverware drawer, where she pulled out a spatula.

"I just… I don't want to see this for you."

She slammed her palm down on the island. "Goddamn it. I just sat there and watched you drink them down, and I never once tried to stop you. Do you know why?"

"Why?"

"Because I need you." She sat down on the island's stool and slid the pills in front of her. "I don't want to do this alone."

Dylan picked up his bottle, twisted the cap, and took a sip. "What are they?"

Hunching over the pills, she used the fat part of the spatula's handle to crush and grind the pills into powder. "Little of this. Little of that."

He walked around the island and rifled through his junk drawer where he kept a stash of Dunkin' Donuts iced coffee straws and a pair of scissors. With a couple of snips, he made a few smaller straws for them to snort with. He held them up to show her. "Will these do?"

Victoria broke the pill's powder down into thin lines. She brushed the hair out of her face, and Dylan nearly fell out of his skin. All the humanity had washed away from her, leaving only the ghost. Her eyes were soaked in hellfire, and her mouth broke into an animalistic snarl. Without a word, she snatched one of the straws from his hand and sucked a line into her nostril. Without hesitation, she did another.

As she looked up at the ceiling, wiping her nose and sniffling, he saw the humanity again, ugly, frayed, and beautiful. Her red eyes cleared like storm clouds, giving way to blue skies, but thin lightning strikes ran through them, and water trickled down her cheeks. "I'm sorry," she said.

He leaned in close to her, bent low, and took a bump. It burned in the back of his nose and throat. He hadn't snorted anything in years, and now he remembered why he hated it so much. To clear the stuffy feeling in his throat, he drank some more vodka.

Victoria stood up and wiped her cheeks. "I'm sorry," she said again.

"Me too."

"What now?"

"I feel like we need music."

She nodded. Her chest moved in dramatic ins and outs, and her breath came in audible gasps as if she'd just run ten laps.

"What should we listen to?" Was he yelling? Techno-style thumps filled the room. Maybe they already had music?

Whatever happened next failed to stick in Dylan's mind. There were moments, but most of it peeled off like dirty tape. More snorting. More drinking. Victoria dancing on the island. Music. God, it was so loud. How did the neighbors not complain? Sweating. Hearts galloping like horses riding into the apocalypse.

Hours ticked by, and as far as Dylan remembered, it was just partying. And then the look came, collapsing the black outs, and everything after that look would never leave his mind. No more dirty tape. The rest of the night would stick to his brain with hammered-in nails.

They were dancing on his mattress, music blaring from the television. Victoria stopped to pull her hair back, and her fiery red eyes locked onto his as she shouted, "I'm hungry."

And fuck he was hungry too.

Her sweat made the mesh top of her dress cling to her flesh, and her skin glistened underneath. She breathed heavily, showing her ribs on each inhale. "I think we've avoided it long enough," she said.

He pushed her against the wall, and she leaped up, wrapping her legs around his waist. One of her hands dug into his hair, and her tongue went into his mouth. He moved his head and kissed her neck while his hand slid down her back, unzipping her dress.

Her legs left his waist, and she pushed him back a few inches. He watched as she dropped her dress to her ankles.

"Take it out. I want to see it," she said.

He unzipped his jeans and pulled his dick out, already hard and pulsing.

Within seconds, her bra and underwear hit the floor, and she pushed on Dylan's chest, making him fall onto the mattress. He could have sworn his body hit two seconds before his soul did.

She jumped on top of him and wasted no time putting him inside her. No foreplay. She just wanted to fuck.

As soon as he went inside her, everything changed. He no longer felt the varying degrees of electricity, and instead, the Earth rocked off its access and drove straight toward the sun. His skin burned, and his insides felt like they were melting. Agonizing.

She pinned his shoulders down with her hands and rotated her hips. Blood rushed to his head, a volcanic eruption of pleasure and pain and sweltering fear. Dylan curled his fingers, trying to grip the sheets under him, but felt nothing. He tried again, but again, found nothing. He swatted behind him, and his hand met only cold air.

In a panic, he turned his head away from her and saw the television at eye level, despite it being on top of a stand.

"What's happening?" he asked.

She moved hard and fast, riding up and down on him. Sweat poured from her body, and her wet hair clung to her forehead and cheeks.

"What's happening?" he asked again, and noticed they were now above the television.

She moaned and went faster. He'd never felt anything like it before. It was intense pleasure, but it hurt so badly, like a poison coursing through his blood, an infection, a disease, rendering his muscles useless, entropy, catatonia, rot, searing flesh, boiling organs, parasitic chewing, death. Death.

DEATH! And still, he needed to cum, his body screaming for it, desperate to load Victoria up with him. It was like they were not two strangers collapsing into one another, but each the blade on a pair of scissors, destined to meet and cut and cut and cut until the entire world was just a pile of shredded fragile paper pieces.

He leaned up, wrapping his arms around her, and her upper body collided with his, and they rolled until he was on top. Vertigo hit as he saw the distance between him and the floor, and then boom, his back hit the ceiling.

And now he led the action, slamming into her over and over. She scratched his back and bit his shoulder so hard it drew blood. He hollered in pain, and she pulled away smiling at him with a crimson lips, droplets of his blood streaming from her mouth to her chin.

He hollered and reached for the floor. It was so far away.

And then his muscles spasmed, everything tightened, and he exploded inside her. She ripped at his hair and screamed a pleasurable howl. Still inside her, their bodies slowly lowered to the mattress. He pulled out of her, rolled over, and they both panted, staring at the ceiling. His body was slick with sweat. The pain subsided, all but in his chest, where a throbbing ache hammered at his ribs.

"What was that?" he asked, knowing she'd never answer.

"That was the storm. And now we rest until we can tally the destruction." Her voice was not her own.

With all of the pain and enjoyment removed, he felt nothing but terror. She rolled over and put her sweat-soaked arm across his chest, nuzzling her head between his arm and torso. Her finger twisted gently at his chest hair.

He found it soothing, despite the growing dread building in his stomach.

She stayed that way for a long time, neither of them moving or talking.

"I just want to be happy," she whispered. "I forgot what it feels like."

He said nothing. His eyelids gained weight and pulled down on him, but his mind screamed, *Please, no. Do not fall asleep. You cannot fall asleep.*

Victoria noticed somehow and said, "Aren't you afraid to fall asleep? What if you never wake up?"

"Why would you say that?" he asked.

She shrugged. "I don't know. I think about that all the time. Besides, you have a complete stranger on top of you. Who knows what I could do?" She lifted her head an inch and offered him a sly smile. "I wouldn't fall asleep if I were you. I may just kill you."

You may. You are, he thought. But just like he couldn't resist her demands all night, he couldn't fight the desperate need to sleep now. Maybe she did that, too, with her gentle caressing of his skin and hair. She lulled him. His eyes shut, and he opened them in a panic, heart racing. *Don't go to sleep.*

He somehow knew if he passed out, it was over. He'd never wake up. She'd finish her plans and devour him. She owned him now.

Do not fall asleep.

Do not.

Stay awake.

Stay awake, dammit.

His head dropped to the side, muscles easing, heartrate steadying. The drum of the world slipped into a slow metronome.

Fight this, Dylan.

Fight it.

Somewhere in the echoing void of the world between sleep and reality, Victoria sang, "Don't fall asleep. Don't leave me alone to my own devices."

His eyes shut and wouldn't open. A cold breeze took the

spots where Victoria's head and arm had been. She no longer lay on top of him. She was going to kill him now. It was time.

And he collapsed into the depths of drunken sleep.

Birds.

Motors running.

Footsteps thudding above him.

Dylan opened his eyes. His head ached instantly, and his throat hurt. He coughed.

The sun leaked through the drapes, and he had to squint to see. "What the fuck?"

It took a few minutes for his mind to wrap around the events leading him here. He drank last night. His body hurt. He knew he was too old to avoid a hangover, but it surprised him how much it felt like the ones he got near the end, the ones that surpassed a normal hangover because they fit more squarely in the realm of detoxing. It had been ten years since he'd last had a drink, so detoxing wasn't possible, but it sure felt like it.

Then he remembered snorting pills. Lord knows which ones. Victoria. He quickly turned his head, and there she lay, her back to him, wrapped in a thin blue sheet, feet sticking out the bottom.

Dear God, what a weird night, he thought. He remembered the way her eyes turned red, the way she touched his forehead to diminish his drunkenness, the way they floated during sex, and he wondered what the hell kind of drugs he'd done. He'd never heard of hallucinations so insane or intense.

He crawled out of his side of the bed and went to the kitchen, where he poured himself a glass of cold water. He gulped it down, praying to rid himself of the dehydration.

He glanced at the bag of pills on the table, still loaded with plenty more in there. It made him sad. Would she use them? Now that he had the morning to feel it out, he thought he might be at that Monday meeting after all. Maybe he could convince her to join him. Maybe they could even go together.

He stayed in the kitchen for a while, drinking another glass of water, not wanting to wake the poor girl up. He wondered how much later she stayed up, and what she did in that time. From the looks of it, she didn't take any more pills, or maybe just one or two. The vodka might be lower in the bottle, but not by much.

If he felt like a truck had hit him, how would she feel when she woke up? Would she regret their encounter? He wondered if they would date, or talk further, or if this was it. One night.

He turned on the coffee pot, in case she'd want some when she woke up, but he personally couldn't stand coffee after a night of drinking. It had always been that way. His heart couldn't handle it.

After a while, he talked himself into waking her up to offer her breakfast. He wanted something in his system and thought she might like it too. When he came into the living room, he talked himself out of the truth. He saw it as soon as he glanced at her face, but he refused to accept it. Her lips were purplish, her skin a waxy white.

"Victoria?"

He ran to her side, dropping to his knees, and shook her. Her body rocked with his movements, lifeless.

"Victoria?" He shook her harder. Her chest wasn't moving. He put his hand in front of her mouth; no air coming out.

"No. No. No. Wake up!" he yelled loudly.

"Fuck." He ran to the phone, calling 911. He rambled to them, explaining what happened. As soon as he hung up, he grabbed the pills and flushed them down the toilet but kept the liquor bottles on the island.

"Oh fuck. Oh my God." He paced around the room. Tears formed in his eyes. "Victoria, please get up. I need you to get up, okay." He wasn't a fucking doctor. Maybe he had it wrong.

The police and EMTs came, entering his apartment. He sat on the island and retold the story of his night, minus the pills, and the magic.

They asked him the same questions repeatedly, as if trying to trip him up.

Where did you meet her?

Did she come up to you or did you go up to her?

How did you end up talking?

What did you talk about?

Who approached whom?

Where did you first meet her?

As he talked to them, his headache rose to unbearable levels, and his stomach spun like a washing cycle. The EMTs placed Victoria on a stretcher and covered her in a white blanket. Her arm flopped off the side. Dylan pictured her last night, dancing with her friends, a poisonous smile on her face, the kind that melts a person's insides.

He thought about her walking the halls of a hospital, bags under her eyes, but happy to be there all the same. He imagined the changes in her face when she had administered the wrong prescription to a child. He heard her bad Morticia Addams imitation, the way her voice leaked out in a squeak when she cried, and the hard, confident way she laughed.

Eventually, everyone left. They took her dress and underwear. Dylan saw them shove the clothes, each item separated, into paper bags. Within the confines of the evidence bag, her cartoonish goth dress looked like nothing more than a black square.

Dylan sat on his mattress and cried. Without the squawks from the police walkie-talkies, and the bustle of EMTs, detectives, and police officers, Dylan had nothing left to accompany him. Just the apparition that caused him to levitate last night, with its red eyes and electric touch. Just him and the ghost.

* * *

When I started this story, I knew what I DIDN'T want it to be. I didn't want it to preach about sobriety or give some kind of stance or feeling on someone losing their battle with it. I just wanted to tell a story where it happens and to get into the minds of those who feel like they can't keep up with it. But I also didn't want it to be a story that anyone could use as an excuse for it. As someone with ten years of sobriety, I often think about what would happen to my life if I ever gave in. The picture of it scares me. This story is me examining the lives of two people who give into their addictions and together, bring themselves down, both using each other to justify it. And of course, in true Gage fashion, it ends tragically for both of them.

DARK ARTS AND SWEETHEARTS

Chaz drove a 1985 Plymouth Reliant, which was quite frankly the single worst vehicle to bring up the slick rain-soaked dirt hill leading toward the Tanner's Switch Fair. Every ten feet or so, he had to course correct as the wheels spun endlessly, the engine roared, and the car slipped forty-five degrees to the left. He freaked out a little. Every spinout brought him dangerously close to smacking the front end of someone coming down the hill on their way out of the fair.

On top of that, when the cars moved in front of him, he had to go from brake to gas instantly or the Reliant would roll backward, and the asshole in the Dodge Neon behind him didn't want to give a centimeter for breathing room.

Worse still was Jess staring at him from the passenger seat. She got a kick out of it, the unruliness of the route, and how the car provided amusement park fun before they even entered the gates, but Chaz didn't want to look like an idiot already. He imagined the conversations with her friends.

"Hey, how did your first date go?"

"Well, let me tell you, the douchebag crashed the car before we got to

do anything. Couldn't even handle a little mud. And, hey, my neck and back hurt."

The traffic in front of them moved forward a foot or so, and Chaz hit the gas and brake in rapid succession, causing him and Jess to jerk forward. But he managed to keep the Reliant facing forward, and didn't roll back into the Neon, or go too far forward into the black Chevy Tahoe.

"We'll get there eventually," he said with an awkward laugh.

Jess said, "What are we gonna do first?"

Chaz raised an eyebrow. "That's up to you."

Jess sat sideways, pulling her feet up on the seat, and resting her knees in the center. That was one of the reasons Chaz loved the old Reliant. It had one long bench seat in the front. No center console in the way. Before Jess, he dated Kristina, and she loved the drive-in movie theaters. With that trusty bench seat, they were able to do all sorts of things in the front. It was a shame they stopped making cars that way. The damn gear shift and change compartment got in the way of companionship.

"Well, I wanna go on the rides and check out the midway, but I really like the little shops, and I know it's silly, but I like to see the kids' arts and crafts tables. I just picture those kids making their art and getting excited knowing people will see it and appreciate it."

Chaz gave her a double take between jerking the car forward another few feet. "Damn, you know a lot about the fair."

She laughed and rolled the gum in her mouth from one side to the other. "Well, I'll tell you a secret."

Chaz wiped his sweaty hands on the side of his shirt before returning them to the wheel. "Oh, okay. Now I'm excited. Am I about to learn some little-known fact about Jess?"

She smiled. "Yeah, kind of. I have ties to this fair. A lot of them."

"Tell me more."

The Reliant jerked forward, getting closer to the turn-in where Chaz would finally get to navigate on level land, albeit bumpy, muddy, grassy, land. At least it wasn't uphill.

"Okay, so, first, I was one of those kids. I used to enter the art contests all the time. Even scored some ribbons. Lots of them, actually. I was a damn good painter when I was seven." She chuckled. "But, also, my mom used to run a table where she made personalized items like lighters, plaques, blah blah. She was all into etching." She giggled some more. "Meanwhile, my auntie was a farmer, so she had shit in the agricultural section, and always had, like, pigs and sheep on display."

Chaz turned the car left, happy to finally get out of the big line. "In other words, your entire family worked at this fair."

She slapped his arm playfully. "I'm not even done. That same aunt, well, her husband ran the line dancing classes. And my cousin worked one of the games in the midway. In fact, he still may. I don't know. I haven't been here in a few years, and I don't really see that side of the family much."

"Jeez, you all really ran the show around here. What game did he run?"

"Oh, it changed all the time. The folks who own those games mainly run as a family operation. They're good people for the most part. A couple of them are weirdos, but most of them are cool. Anyway, they had, like, five or six people outside the family helping them run games, and they switched around who ran what."

"Well, since you know the ins and outs, you can help me figure out which games to play where I won't embarrass myself or get conned. You can walk outta here with a big ole stuffed animal, and I can pretend to be a badass for it."

The wheels hit a mud patch and, for a second, spun out. Chaz freaked out and nailed the gas, which was probably the wrong thing to do, but somehow it managed to get the car moving before Jess noticed anything was wrong. He spotted an open space up ahead but debated on skipping it and driving toward the entrance to see if they could find anything closer, but then he decided having a bit of distance to walk with Jess both before and after the fair wasn't the worst thing in the world, and in fact, it might just be the best.

The space itself was grassy, but behind it was a thick, muddy pool, and Chaz hoped to himself that the car in front of them was gone before they left, because if he had to back up, he'd probably get the car stuck. Although he managed to drive through it when he pulled in, so he should probably stop stressing so damned much.

They had a long dirt path to walk down, passing aisles of cars, before reaching the ticket booth. People passed them coming back to their cars, some of them lugging their exhausted kids and others coming out as couples, holding hands, and carrying bags, but also looking pretty exhausted. Chaz was happy they came in the evening while the sun hid behind the mountains instead of having it hovering over them and beating the energy from their bodies as they waltzed around crafting tables and amusement rides.

Jess held his hand and pointed at the rides looming high and flashing their dazzling lights. Decked-out trucks with cartoonishly large wheels roared and revved behind fencing, reminding Chaz of the type of folks who hung out within the grounds. He had nothing against them, but they weren't his kind of people, either, and he wished the dirt road would stretch out and leave him and Jess holding hands and walking forever.

Near the entrance, people working the fair took breaks and smoked. The smell of cigarettes and weed draped over the wooden shack with the ticket windows like storm clouds.

There wasn't a line to get in, another reason for Chaz to celebrate their late arrival. Teenagers scampered all over the grounds like rats. They laughed and played and hugged and sang. Some looked like good kids. Some looked like pieces of shit. Chaz knew those kinds of assessments weren't nice, but he had trouble with crowds and felt on high alert at all times, ready to fight, run, or prepare for whatever this fucked up world tossed his way.

Jess led him through a couple of barn-style buildings where the fair displayed prize-winning vegetables and artwork. The carrots and squashes didn't impress him much, but some of the artwork blew his mind, especially when he saw the ages of the artists. Kids as young as nine years old were drawing pictures much better than he could.

They looked at cows and pigs and chickens and rabbits, then they headed to the bleachers for the egg toss contest. As they sat there, waiting for the games to begin, Chaz ran his eyes all over, eyeing the spectators, assessing any dangers.

Jess put her arm around his back and rested her head on his shoulder. "I can't tell you how much I love this place."

Chaz pulled her in closer. "I'm glad you do. And I'm glad I get to experience it with you. I feel like you're showing me your history or something."

She wrapped her fingers around his upper arm. "That's what it feels like."

The groups came out in the fenced-in field, and someone separated them about two feet apart from their partners.

"Alright, pick three teams who you think might win, and then I'll pick my teams."

She pulled off him, a smile brimming on her face. "Okay. Okay. Let's play. Are we putting money on this?"

"How about winner gives the other a massage."

"That sounds like you win either way, but whatever. I'm down." She leaned in for a better view of the teams. "I pick the boy-girl couple in the black shirts. The girl wearing the Fair Princess sash with the red-headed partner, aaaaaand those two old dudes right at the end."

Chaz leaned back and crossed his arms around his stomach.

"What?" Jess asked. "Who are you picking?"

Chaz pointed to the middle. "Those two kids right in the middle. Blue shirt and orange shirt."

"Look at you with that confident face. Hell no. You said we pick three."

"I don't need three. Those two kids are winning."

"Why are you so sure?"

He shrugged. "Those kids got it. I can see it in their eyes. They don't fuck around."

A guy in a white shirt and a bow tie came out with a microphone and explained the rules to the participants and the crowd. And with a whistle, the first toss began. Only one team was eliminated, a mom and her five-year-old. Chaz knew they didn't stand a chance, but wished they survived a couple of rounds so the little girl could feel proud.

While they waited for the second toss, Chaz scanned the area again. A man in camo shorts sat alone on a bench doing his own scanning. A couple of kids whispered to one another and looked around all shady. A couple in their fifties argued with a guy at a table selling old comic books. They all put him on alert, but none of them screamed, "WARNING! WARNING! WARNING!"

Each team stepped backward, putting more space between their teammates. One side tossed their eggs. A bunch of teams fell out on round two, leaving about nine teams remaining. All of Jess's teams and Chaz's one team made it through.

Jess clapped. "I still got my three."

Chaz shook his head. "Don't matter. I got this."

He gave a quick glance to the crowd. Camo pants had company now. A woman around his age and two kids. That eased Chaz a little. The two teens were off with a bigger group. Chaz didn't like the looks of any of them, but they were headed to the rides, so he didn't have to worry about them just yet. The couple arguing with the dude at the table was making more of a commotion now, and a few security folks in bright yellow shirts made their way over.

Round three.

With even more space between the teammates, eggs flew all over. Crack, crack, crack. Four teams remained. Jess still hung on to the couple in black and the old dudes. The two kids Chaz bet on stayed strong.

The security guys escorted the couple out, and the two douchebags weren't putting up any kind of fight. Meanwhile, a guitar strummed loudly as someone tested out the instruments on the main stage. Earlier, Chaz checked out the website to see who was playing, hoping he'd catch some act he dug from the 90s like Everclear or The Toadies, but it was some old country dude he had never heard of.

A bunch of folks had made their way to the flat grounds in front of the stage, making it harder for Chaz to pinpoint potential threats.

Round four.

All eggs reached their destinations.

Jess nudged Chaz. "I got two staying strong. Fifty percent chance I win. Wanna double or nothing?"

Chaz looked off at the crowd. "What do you want to add to the bet?"

"If I win, you gotta take one of those old-timey photos with me. If I lose, I'll go home with you tonight."

He whipped his head toward her. "Damn. Double or nothing it is. But even if I win, I'll do the old-timey photo."

Jess cracked her knuckles as if she were the one out there waiting to catch an egg. "Alright. Let's see where I'm sleeping tonight."

Round five.

The man in the black shirt over-tossed his egg to his wife. She gave an impressive dive for it, but it was way too far away.

Three teams remained. Jess and Chaz both had one left in the race.

A lot of the folks waiting for the concert looked like trouble to Chaz, but that might have been his bias toward country music fans.

Round six.

Eggs flew. The old dudes were in sync, and they made Chaz nervous because they were damned good. His kids made it through, but it was a close one. The little man in orange had to reach up to grab the egg and spun his arm to keep the egg from cracking all over his hand. The other remaining team, a young boy and his dad, finally lost when the dad caught the hard-tossed egg on his chest. He shook yolk off his hands as he waltzed away with his smiling son. Chaz enjoyed seeing the pride in their faces for having made it so far.

One more glance at the crowd. Chaz found himself relaxing. Folks just wanted to have a good time. Jess grew up with this crowd, and she was good people. The best kind of people. This was their first date, but they'd worked together for years, and there wasn't another person around that he trusted more.

Round seven. Only two teams remained and the distance between the teammates was ridiculous. Chaz wondered what would happen if both teams lost. He couldn't imagine anyone catching an egg from this far away and it not smashing all over their hands.

The eggs went up. Soaring through the air. Chaz and Jess both stood up.

TatTatTatTatTatTatTat.

People screamed.

TatTatTatTatTatTatTat.

Running.

TatTatTatTatTatTatTat.

Everyone ran in different directions, smashing into each other, knocking each other over.

It took Chaz a minute to realize what happened. Gunshots.

TatTatTatTatTatTatTat.

He grabbed Jess' hand and led her off the bleachers. The shots seemed to come from the entrance area, and most people all ran toward the exit, which was twenty feet from where the shots rang out.

Chaz ran toward the livestock exhibits instead. There, he wouldn't have to battle the crowds, which were dangerous in their own right. Once those people bottlenecked at the exit, they'd be stepping on each other and crushing one another. He'd also be moving away from the shots. The livestock exhibits were in the corner of the fair, and only a small fence blocked them from the wooded area around it. They could easily hide out in there until the situation was resolved.

A long barn stretched for thirty or forty feet, filled with chickens. The folks in that area smartly hopped the fence and hid out in the woods, ducking and yelling to one another to *runrunrun.*

Just as Chaz and Jess reached the area more gunshots rang out, these much closer. Either there was a second shooter, or the man with the gun had made it quite a distance. Chaz doubted the second option. A place like this had a lot of security. Someone would have stopped him by now, but if there were multiple shooters, who knew how much death they could cause before it all ended?

TatTatTatTatTatTatTat.

The shots were too close to risk going for the fence. Instead, Chaz veered left, leading them deeper into the fair. Jess lagged behind, but he kept his hand latched with hers. Pockets of people ran toward the exit from the midway, but the bulk of them had already passed where Chaz went. A few folks smashed into Chaz as they ran, but there weren't enough of them to knock him over and crush him.

The bulbs flashed from the rides. Red, yellow, and green

lights danced up and down the spokes of the Ferris wheel. White lights circled the carts on the Zipper. Chaz pulled Jess toward the long stretch of game booths, figuring they could run behind them until they reached the outer fencing, where they could escape down toward the road.

When they veered behind the booths, one of the game workers, wearing his bright purple "Midway Machinations Inc." shirt, grabbed Chaz's shirt and shoved him against the wall. Chaz lost his grip on Jess' hand.

"What the hell are you doing?"

The man put his finger to Chaz's mouth. "Shhhhh."

Jess said with shaky breath, "That's my cousin."

Chaz looked ~~to~~ at Jess and, for the first time, saw that she'd been shot. Blood soaked her shoulder and stomach. She hunched over, clutching the wound in her gut.

He pushed her cousin off him and ran to her. "What happened?" he asked, realizing how dumb the question was after saying it.

TatTatTatTatTatTatTat. More gunshots, but they were far away. It sounded like a fucking warzone out there.

Jess fell over, collapsing into Chaz. He gently laid her in the dirt. "Fuck. We need to get an ambulance."

Her cousin pushed Chaz off and kneeled down, pressing his hand over Jess' stomach wound. The man was tall and lanky, with long, clumpy hair. He had a long, gaunt face with a bird nose. His chin was peppered in unshaven scraggle that looked more like dirt than hair. And his skin was as pale as the Zipper lights.

"What would you do to save her?" he asked.

Chaz stared at the blood, the way it pumped out, and through her cousin's fingers. "Ah. Anything?"

This was their first date. He'd known her for a long time, and they were best friends at work. He wasn't in love. But he didn't need to be. He would have given the same answer if it were anyone lying there dying.

"Good. I'm going to hold you to that," her cousin said.

"Okay. Just tell me what to do."

More gunshots went off. He imagined, at this point, the police were having a standoff with the shooters. He prayed to God the killers weren't still having a field day on the crowds. Luckily, tucked behind the game booths, they weren't seeing anyone else, neither crowds nor shooters.

Her cousin turned his head toward Chaz. His eyes glazed over. "There are dark spirits at these fairgrounds."

Chaz didn't give a shit what this dude thought about the shooters or the fairgrounds. "Let's just help her. Should we try to carry her out to the road and call for help?"

The man shook his head slowly. "Dark spirits feed on the chaos. They're getting stronger. We can use them to help us."

Oh, shit. This fucker is crazy. That's not gonna help, Chaz thought.

The man put his blood-soaked hand in his pocket and pulled out a necklace. "Put this on."

Chaz grabbed it from him, not to play along, but to get the dude to put his hand back on the wound. The necklace was black beaded. A pendant dangled from the center that looked like a tooth with a star etched into it.

"We don't have time for this."

"Just put it on," her cousin snapped.

Chaz scoffed and tossed it around his head. "There. Happy? Now get out of the way. I'm taking her to the road."

Her cousin turned to Chaz, pinning his eyes on him so harshly Chaz could *feel* it. "She's dead my friend. The road ain't gonna help her. Do you know what happens on these fairgrounds during the rest of the year? When the chaos is gone?"

Chaz gave the man a gentle shove. "Get out of my way."

"The spirits of those who died on these grounds turn dark."

When there isn't an active shooter, how many people die here? Chaz thought.

"They live here in the darkness, and they grow more poisoned by the day."

"STOP!" Chaz went to push the man again, but this time Jess' cousin was ready for it, and he grabbed Chaz by the wrists.

He turned his head up and yelled, "A SOUL FOR A SOUL!"

Thunder. Lightning lit the skies.

"A SOUL FOR A SOUL."

He let go of Chaz's wrists as another bolt landed in the midway, creating a boom so loud it shook the grounds. Jess' cousin's hand slapped hard against Chaz's forehead.

"A SOUL FOR A SOUL."

Chaz fell back from the impact, slamming against the back of a booth. In the quick second that passed between the slap and the back of his skull hitting the wood, he saw his own body standing where he'd been. Then it dropped. And the world turned black.

He came to just a second later, but he was in a daze. The world had fogged over. Jess sat up and Chaz wanted to yell to her, to tell her to relax and wait for emergency personnel to arrive.

She glanced around in a daze of her own and then wiped at the site of the gunshot wound in her stomach. Chaz wondered how she managed to prop herself up with a shoulder that had taken a bullet.

"What did you do?" she said to her cousin.

"I saved you," he said and stood up, wiping his knees of the gravel.

Jess turned and looked down. Chaz followed her gaze and noticed his body still lying there like it had been before he passed out. Was he dreaming?

Jess gasped and ran to his body. "What did you do?" she asked again.

"What did you want me to do? You were dying. Do you love this guy or something?"

"No. But I never asked for you to do this. My life isn't more important than anyone else's, and you probably just damned us both."

Her cousin seemed unconcerned. "You'll thank me tomorrow."

Chaz leaned forward, examining his own body. That's when he saw the blood gushing from his stomach. He looked up. Jess was caked in blood, but no more poured from her stomach or her shoulder.

"No," Chaz said. He slowly rose to his feet. "There's no fucking way."

He looked left and right. Everything looked gray. There was no sounds spilling from the rides and games. No more gunshots or screams, or even midway music.

He panicked. "What the fuck?"

He stepped toward Jess, slowly putting his shaking hand forward. If he went to touch her and his hand passed through her, he'd know he was a ghost, that he was dead.

His hand inched toward her arm, wanting to know, but also not wanting to know at all.

Finally, his fingertips touched her skin, and he felt it. Thank God. She must have, too, because she looked in his direction and rubbed her hand where he'd touched.

"Do you see me?" he asked.

"Chaz?"

He smiled. "Yes. What's happening?"

Her cousin moved closer to her. "Did you feel him?"

She nodded. "Chaz, are you still here? If so, touch me again."

So, she couldn't see him. He placed his hand on her upper arm. She gasped and tears filled her eyes. What was happening? Was he dead? Was this a Patrick Swayze, Demi Moore situation?

"Chaz. You're still here." She smiled and then it quickly sunk into a frown. "Chaz, you need to run. You need to get the hell out of here, now!"

His heart sank. He knew it was silly to feel offended considering the circumstances, but it happened, nonetheless. What did she mean?

Something banged, breeding a hollow thud into the dark gray sky. Once. Twice. Three times. Thud. Thud. Thud.

He turned toward the sound coming from the end of the game booths. A man stood, partially shrouded in the gloom. His silhouette showed his husky build and gigantic height. He must have been 280 pounds and 6'7". The man slammed his fist on the wooden booth.

He yelled. At first, Chaz thought he was howling at the moon, but the man said, "Neeeeeeeeeeewwwwwwwwwwwwwwww blood."

Chaz knew he should run, but how could he look away? He had no idea what world he'd entered or how it operated. He'd spent years formulating a pattern, a way to understand the environment around him. He was careful about what he ate, worked out four times a week. He left early for work, so he didn't have to drive fast.

And now he stood in a world made of grays with his body just a few feet from his... what? Soul? He didn't even know. Was this death or some kind of parallel world?

The Giant tested the waters, playfully putting one foot in front of the other. He kept one arm behind his back. Chaz wished he could see the man's face, his features. Was he friend or foe?

The answer came a few seconds later when The Giant moved his hand out from behind his back and launched something toward Chaz. The wooden back to the booth on Chaz's side made a THUNG sound, and Chaz slowly turned his head to see a knife handle sticking out of the wood.

He turned his head back to The Giant, who stood still, waiting to see how Chaz would react to what was clearly a threat. Chaz put one foot back, then spun and ran.

The Giant's feet smacked against the ground. Chaz ran out onto the midway, debating on where to go. Just outside the games and rides was a small barn with three doors. It was where they displayed the antique farming equipment, but Chaz was only concerned with getting into a hiding spot that had multiple places of egress.

As he ran across the midway, The Giant's steps continued charging, getting closer with each stomp. For such a husky person, he was incredibly fast. Chaz ran 5ks, and kept a good speed, so he couldn't believe The Giant could keep up. He wanted to get back to Jess and her cousin, to push them for answers, but he couldn't think of a single way to get to them without getting far the fuck away from The Giant first.

Chaz made his way to the Ferris wheel. The Giant's footsteps were too close. He'd never make it to the barn, so he chanced a climb. Big man could run, but could he carry that weight up the Ferris wheel spokes?

First, Chaz hopped the metal bars designed to keep the lines wrapping around instead of piling out and blocking the midway. When he jumped the last one, he used the controller's station for a boost and launched himself onto the bottom cart. It rocked back and forth as he landed on top of it.

Before he jumped to the spokes, he gave a glance toward The Giant to see if the man was following him. He wasn't, but he stood right by the controller's station, staring up at Chaz. For the first time, Chaz saw the man's features. He wore overalls with a greasy yellow shirt underneath. He was bald and shiny on the top of his head, but he had thick, matted hair wrapped around his skull on the sides and back.

But it was his face that would haunt Chaz for the rest of

his life. The man's mouth stretched unnaturally long, curling up the cheeks all the way to his temples, and he had two sets of teeth, one behind the other. The ones in the back were longer and more visible, and they curved down like sickles.

Chaz turned away, wincing, and jumped up to the spokes.

"Please, make him leave. Make him leave," Chaz whispered to himself as he climbed.

He eyed a cart hanging at the Ferris wheel's forty-five-degree mark. It was low enough to the ground where if he fell, he wouldn't die. He could fuck up his legs if he didn't land right, but he wouldn't die. And it was tall enough that if The Giant didn't climb, he wasn't going to reach Chaz.

The spokes were thick, so Chaz could get good footing on them as he slid to the side. Something dinged against the metal, and he nearly slipped. He glanced back to see the man holding a knife. The man flicked his wrist, and the knife flew at Chaz, forcing him to lift his foot, which in turn nearly made him lose his balance. The man shook his hand, and another knife appeared.

"Well, shit." Chaz gripped one spoke with his hands and slid down another. Again, a knife clanged against the metal.

The cart he moved toward shook. He nearly screamed when a pair of eyes appeared behind the latticed metallic back of the cart.

"Hurry, I'll get you in," a voice inside the cart said. It was soft, and a little high-pitched.

Chaz slid faster, not really trusting the voice, but out of options otherwise.

The Giant threw another knife and hit the bottom of Chaz's shoe. The action made Chaz realize the guy was intentionally missing. He just wanted to knock Chaz down.

"Neeeeeewwwwwwwwwwwwww blood," The Giant shouted, all yeehaw and taunting.

As Chaz reached the cart, the front gate popped open. "Get in!" the voice said.

Chaz hopped in the cart, the door slammed shut, and a knife clanged against the metal.

He got a look at the person who'd helped him. A small child. The kid was dressed in an ugly brown checkered button-down, and jeans rolled up at the bottom.

"Better watch out for The Farmer," the boy said.

"That's what you call him? I've been calling him The Giant."

The boy smiled. "That works too. Anyway, you don't want to stay on his bad side. He's one of the meanest."

"One of?"

The boy laughed. "Want to see them all?"

"Not really. What is this place?"

The boy frowned. "I don't know. But I've been here a really long time. You have to hide a lot, or they'll make you just like them, but it's not all bad."

"How many of them are there?"

He smiled again. "I'll show you." The boy leaned forward and put his fingers through the latticed frame. With a deep breath, he closed his eyes, and his fingers started to glow. The entire Ferris wheel shook and squeaked, and then cheap piano music kicked in and the ride started going.

Chaz's eyes grew wide. "What are you doing? We're gonna go right by The Giant."

The boy sat in the cart's seat and shook his head. "He can't come in here. They all have a range. No one can get on the Ferris wheel."

The cart passed the base, where The Giant stood staring with a scrunched face, holding a knife in front of his layers of teeth.

As it went up, Chaz laughed at his fear of heights. It kicked in, even now when he faced much bigger threats, and he was dead already anyway, so what difference did it make?

When the cart reached the pinnacle of the wheel, the boy did his trick again and made the ride stop. Chaz looked out to behind the games. Jess and her cousin were gone. He wondered if they found safety from the shooter. Had they left the park?

"What are you looking at?" the boy asked.

"My friend was down there. She must have left."

"You stop being able to see them after you've been here for a little bit."

"Oh."

"But you can see people sometimes when they're laughing or having a lot of fun. During the fair, you get to see a lot of people. I always hope one day I'll see my mom and dad again. But they'll probably never come back here since it's where their son died."

Chaz turned to the boy. "What happened to you?"

He rocked his butt in his seat, causing the cart to shake. "Fell off the Ferris wheel. Duh."

"Damn. I'm sorry."

"They used to be open. The carts, I mean. They were open, and I unbuckled and leaned off to act tough to my older brother. Slipped right out. Now they put this weird fence stuff around it."

"How long ago was that?"

The boy shrugged.

"What year was it?" Chaz thought that might help.

"1985?"

Jesus. Chaz's heart sank. It wasn't just that the boy had died decades ago, but that he'd spent all those years locked away on the very ride that brought him here in the first place.

"So, what happens here? When someone dies in the park, they stay here? And people like The Giant turn them into bad guys?"

"Kind of. Their darkness makes it so other people die. It leaks into the real world."

A realization hit Chaz. "Someone opened fire on the fair. There's probably a lot of new dead in here tonight."

The boy looked out at the park. "We need to get to them first. We can help them."

"Kid, we gotta keep ourselves safe first."

The boy turned to Chaz. "I don't want to be alone anymore."

Damn. He didn't know what to say, so he stared out at the fairgrounds. If the world wasn't gray and misty, it would have been beautiful. The aerial view showed the splendid layout of the shops and rides and concert area and fields. It was spectacular. But it was also horrifying because Chaz saw movement. A lot of it. Dark spirits everywhere.

"Will you help me?" The boy put his hand in Chaz's.

Chaz closed his eyes and gasped, "Yeah, kid. Yeah, I will."

The boy smiled. "I'm Kenny, by the way."

"Chaz."

"Hi, Chaz. Do you like Thundercats?"

"Hell yeah, I do. Now, how do we get around The Giant?"

The boy pointed to the ground. "Giant's gone. He'll be around, looking for new blood, but you have some time, and he can't leave the midway, so you just need to get out of here."

"Cool. I'll run to that antique barn." He nodded toward it.

The kid laughed. "You definitely do not want to go in there. That's where The Seamstress is."

"So, what do I do?"

The boy navigated with his finger, following the pathways through the fairgrounds. "Go through the shops. You won't find much there. Then you'll need to go through the field by the stage. There's a bad guy in there, but he's old and useless. I call him The Roadie, because he was a roadie for The Bellamy Brothers. He got in a fight with a fan and got stabbed."

"How do we know where all the new people are? The ones that got shot?"

The boy pointed toward the exit. "They'll all be trying to get out. Trust me, they'll crowd that gate for days before it clicks that they will never be able to leave."

That made the hairs on the back of Chaz's neck stand up. He will never get out.

"Plus, right near the exit gate is a fenced-in area where they do line dancing, and that's one of the worst spots. Ten of them died in one year, all from heat stroke. Be careful over there. Anyway, all the new people would have seen the line dancing area and that would have made them panic and try to get out. The gate area itself is safe."

Chaz shook his head. "Okay, so boom, boom, boom. Run through the shops, hit the field where I'll have to avoid an old roadie dude, and be careful at the line dancing. Then I'll get them all at the gates. What do I do when I got them?"

"Come back here. We're safe on the Ferris wheel."

"And I'm guessing you aren't coming with me. Are you stuck on here?"

The boy nodded.

Chaz hated that even in death he could feel the beginnings of a panic attack. "Okay, well, bring this thing back down, and I'll get going."

Kenny shook his head. "No can do. If I make the ride move, the music will come on and alert The Giant. You gotta climb down."

"If I fall, will I die? I mean, die again? Is that possible?"

"Nah. The only way to die again is if one of them out there kills you."

"So, I can just jump off this thing and be alright?"

Kenny laughed. "No, dummy. You can still feel pain. And if you break your leg, you won't be able to run. And you're gonna need to run. Probably a lot."

"Okay, well I should go because thinking about it is making me sick."

Kenny opened the door, and Chaz glanced around,

making sure The Giant wasn't around. He didn't like that he couldn't see The Giant *anywhere,* but at least he wasn't in the near vicinity.

He slid down the first spoke on his ass, using the heel of his feet to stop him from free falling. From the center, he had an easier time. He crawled along a spoke going ninety degrees and hopped on the cart at the end of it. Using the latticed metal, he climbed down the cart and jumped from it to the next one down. His feet made a light DING noise when he landed and he winced, but it didn't seem to attract The Giant.

Using the latticed metal, he climbed to the bottom of the cart, and from there, he was able to drop down without hurting himself. But being back on the ground made him feel exposed. He wasted no time, running toward the shops.

As soon as he passed the midway, he took a breath and relaxed a little, until a thought hit him. What other spirits roamed this place that weren't in the spots Kenny mentioned? One wrong move could put him in the arms of some other ridiculous dark monster.

He walked along the path where the shops flanked him on each side, keeping alert. He knew what the kid told him, but it didn't ease his concern any. When he reached the concert field, he scanned the area for The Roadie. There was no sign of him.

Large oak trees dotted the edges of the field, and Chaz used them for cover, making a wide arc around the stage. But the trees ended right on the side of the stage, and he'd have to cross the front of it to make it to the other side. He supposed he could go behind it, but that put him outside the realm of the field, and he'd rather face the devil he knew of than one he didn't.

He debated on whether he should run for it, or creep nice and slow to not alert The Roadie. He opted for a middle ground, and power walked. He checked out the stage, wondering if The Roadie hid behind the curtain. As he eyed it, the force of a train slammed into him.

He fell over and tried to push The Roadie off him. The spirit must have been hiding on the roof above the stage and jumped off right as Chaz passed by him.

The man was rabid, a ball of energy. Could spirits be coked out? He shook his head violently, gnashing his teeth and growling. Chaz pushed on the man's chest, keeping his teeth at a distance.

The two rolled on the ground, The Roadie trying to get his teeth closer, and Chaz just trying to separate from him. The Roadie was tall and gaunt. His nose hooked like a bird's beak. When his mouth opened, small puffs of smoke came out. He had long, slick black hair and it kept getting in Chaz's eyes.

Chaz rolled on top and swung his fist, connecting with The Roadie's jaw. And that was that. The Roadie's eyes closed, and his body went limp.

Chaz stood up, catching his breath. While the endeavor scared the shit out of him and stole his wind, the kid had been right. The Roadie was weak.

"Alright, now I just have the friggin' line dancers."

Something itched at his brain, but he couldn't place it. It was something the boy had said that didn't make sense, but try as he might, the problem wouldn't become clear.

He stepped out of the field toward the entrance. On the way, he glanced at the area where the egg drop contest had happened. He eyed the bleachers where he and Jess had sat. Not too long ago, he was having a great first date. Now he was dead, trading his life for hers. He had to admit, he doubted he'd make the same choice twice.

As he walked along the fencing, he heard a small crack. Doing a double take, he caught the source. Two women in their twenties stood about fifteen feet apart, tossing eggs to one another. They both wore white boots and jean shorts that barely covered their asses. One of them had a snake tattoo twisting up her leg.

Chaz wondered how they died and if it happened during the egg toss, or if they just died in that area and decided to take up the traditions of the field.

They never caught each other's eggs. Never even tried. The eggs went up in a big arc and slapped down on the ground in front of them, on their bodies, on the tops of their heads. And they just kept tossing to one another. Endlessly. It was horrific to watch. Like the punishment in a layer of hell.

"Damn," he whispered to himself.

At the same time, both women jerked their heads in his direction and screeched. Within seconds, they flew toward him and slammed themselves into the fencing. Chaz jumped back.

The women clawed at the fence, trying to get out.

Chaz ran. He was almost there, and those women showed him what a distraction could cost him.

The line dancing area was blocked in with a wooden white fence. It was low, just two thick boards wrapping around the area. The ten dancers stood in the center of it, and they were moving. A bigger man with a thick brown beard and a black cowboy hat shouted out steps. "Left then right. Rock step. Point. Swivel."

Chaz made sure to leave some space between him and the fence as he crept around it toward the front entrance.

"Pivot turn. And step and step and step and step."

The back of his legs touched the cold metal of the bleachers.

"Stomp. Stomp. Step and step and step and…"

Chaz slid sideways, keeping his eyes on the spirits.

"…step and step and kill him."

All ten spirits broke from their positions and charged. Luckily, he had a good five feet between him and the fence.

Or so he thought it was lucky until the two older women in the front hopped right over it.

"Oh fuck," he said.

He turned and climbed the bleachers, and the ping-pang of footsteps followed behind him. When he reached the top, he jumped off, but something grabbed his foot in midair. He fell face-first into the ground, and yeah, the kid was right. It fucking hurt.

A body landed on top of him and clawed at his back. His skin burned as nails drove down his spine.

He pushed forward, kicking his feet and finding purchase on someone's face. As soon as he hit the dirt path, the line dancers stopped. They all stared at him along the line of grass which seemingly stopped them from proceeding.

The man in the cowboy hat yelled, "Back home!"

And just like that, they all turned and walked back to the line dancing arena.

Chaz stayed in place, catching his breath yet again, staring in bewilderment as the group of ten lined back up and followed the instructions from the caller.

He stood up, shook his head, and went to the exit. Just like Kenny predicted, a group of eight or so folks stood at the gate, pushing on the fencing and yelling to get out. There were three women, four men, and a small child no older than four. His blood boiled thinking about the mysterious shooter who cut all those lives short.

"Hey," Chaz shouted.

They all twisted to look at him, and then quickly turned back to the fencing and shook it with more force. "Let us out!" one of them screamed.

"I'm not one of them," he said. "I'm here to help you."

A man with a buzzcut gave Chaz his attention. "What do you mean? How can you help? We're dead, aren't we?"

Chaz put his hand up, trying to slow the man down. "Listen, I don't know a lot more than you do, but I think so. I died when y'all did. But I know those things all have a realm. They can't cross it. And I met a boy on the midway who's been here a long time, and he sent me to get you all to meet him by the Ferris wheel."

As Chaz talked, more of the group turned to hear him out.

"I don't know if anything can be done for us. But I know those spirits aren't good, and this kid seems to know the best way to avoid them."

It clicked then. The question that danced around his brain from all Kenny had said. The spirits have realms. Kenny himself had a realm. So why was Chaz able to move around freely? Why would the shooting victims be able to follow him?

He didn't have time to figure it out. He needed to get them to the boy. Maybe it was a mistake. Kenny said the gate was safe, so why drag them through threat after threat just to bring them to the Ferris wheel? Chaz knew the answer. Because the boy was alone and he'd been alone for decades, and Chaz couldn't think of anything worse. In life, he'd feared nothing more. Being alone.

The group of gunshot victims debated following Chaz and came to the consensus they should go with him. The battle was halfway won. Now he just had to get them back to the Ferris wheel.

They ran past the line dancers quickly, avoiding the close call he'd had on the way. When they reached the field, he stopped them.

"Okay, there's a guy in here who's pretty rough." He pointed toward a woman with a ponytail who held the child. "Protect them at all costs. This guy acts feral, but he's easy to drop, so the rest of us need to be prepared to fight."

A short man in a red button-down stepped back. "Why would we go that way?" He pointed toward a wide path. "This way is shorter."

He didn't wait for Chaz to respond and just started walking away. The rest of the group followed immediately.

Chaz ran to get in front of them. "No wait. This way isn't safe."

But by the time they stopped to listen, they were all on the open path between the food booths and the arts and crafts exhibit barn.

And three men came out of nowhere, running on all fours, surrounding the group. People screamed.

Without hesitation, the attackers jumped on the newly dead, ripping into them with their teeth. Chaz had one mission on his mind. He grabbed the child from the lady with the ponytail and ran. He wasn't going to risk saving the rest of them. They should have listened.

Unfortunately, the route to the field was now blocked, and Chaz would have to risk taking the wide path all the way to the midway.

A few of the gunshot victims got away, but the rest were ripped to shreds. Chaz listened to their screams as he dashed down the path. The midway wasn't too far away. The toddler bawled his eyes out while Chaz ran with him.

Two more men jumped down from atop the arts and crafts exhibit.

"Shit!" Chaz yelled.

One of them ran with insane speed, especially since he darted on all fours. Chaz had no choice but to duck into the next barn down. Two of the shooting victims made it into the barn with him, a man and a woman. The rest were all dead.

Dead dead.

The spider-walking spirits came to the doors of the barn, growling and showing their pointed teeth.

They were trapped. He turned slowly, rocking the toddler as the kid sobbed into Chaz's shoulder. Rusty machinery surrounded them. He hadn't realized where they'd gone. In the heat of the moment, he'd just dipped into the nearest place away from the spirits outside.

They were in the antique barn.

"Oh, shit," Chaz said.

"What?" the woman asked.

Chaz shook his head. "Nothing. We need to get out of here as soon as possible. What's your name?"

"Julia," she said.

The man stepped forward. He had a gross goatee and Chaz hated looking at it. "I'm Craig."

Chaz nodded. "I'm Chaz. Listen, this barn isn't safe, but those things are at all the exits. You saw what they did to the others. This is why it's important to listen to me. If we went through the field, we would have been safe. Can you both promise to listen to me?"

They nodded, but honestly, Chaz had no idea what to do now. His plans had ended.

Someone cackled. They all looked everywhere, trying to find the source. But the laughter moved, bouncing from one corner of the barn to another with impossible speed.

"What the hell is that?" Julia asked.

"It's The Seamstress," Chaz said. "Kenny warned me about her."

The cackling traveled from the far side of the barn right toward them, hiding behind the large rusty machines. Then it stopped. The quiet was horrifying. Something squeaked. A gentle noise. They all turned to it. A large, rusty piece of equipment moved onto the walkway where they all stood. It had two big wheels on both sides, and between the them was a long metal bar with blades cycling around it. It moved forward a few inches, the blades spinning.

They all stared, waiting for the machine to roll toward them and kill them all, but it stayed in place.

Craig screamed. They turned to see The Seamstress wrapped around him from behind. One of her hands clawed into his chest with her long, sharp nails. With the other hand, she pulled a needle and thread through Craig's lips.

His screaming turned into mumbles as she sewed his lips

shut. He struggled, but she was too strong. Chaz and Julia ran to the barn exit, where The Spider-Walkers remained, still growling and waiting to pounce.

They were stuck. Chaz turned back to the horror as The Seamstress ran her claws down Craig's chest. Blood and guts spilled from his body. She hummed a song as she continued to sew Craig's face. His lips were pinned shut, and she'd moved onto his eyes.

"We need to get the hell out of here before that happens to us," Chaz said. The toddler cried and screamed, which meant even if they got past The Spider-Walkers, they'd never get through the midway without alerting The Giant.

The bladed machine squeaked again and then rolled forward. It started a little slowly, and then sped up, flying toward Craig and The Seamstress. Before it reached them, The Seamstress hopped onto the ceiling, clinging to it with her long claws.

Chaz shielded the toddler's eyes as the blades slammed into Craig, and blood splattered across the barn.

Julia screamed and ran. She'd seen enough. Using her shoulder, she dove into The Spider-Walkers, trying to knock them over, but it didn't work. Instead, they grabbed her and held her up. As their teeth neared her, Chaz took her cue and gave them a second shoulder.

The two Spider-Walkers and Julia fell to the cement, and Chaz took off running, praying to himself that he gave Julia a fighting chance to get away. The toddler bawled even harder. It rang out like a siren, calling all the dark spirits.

Julia caught up to him. It turned out she was incredibly fast and she overtook him in seconds. Two more Spider-Walkers came from one of the other barn doors, and just before Chaz could reach the midway, one of them grabbed his arm. Julia turned just in time, spun, grabbed the toddler before he could fall, and swatted her foot at the Spider-Walker.

Chaz stepped forward onto the midway, and The Spider-Walkers stayed where they were, unable to cross over. Chaz and Julia didn't have time to pause, not with The Giant out there, so they kept running for the Ferris wheel. Halfway there, the ground shook, and The Giant appeared from behind The Orbiter.

"Run. Run as fast as you can," Chaz yelled to Julia.

And run she did. Even with the toddler in her arms, she outpaced Chaz by a long shot.

They reached the base of the Ferris wheel, and the bottom cart's door swung open. They all piled in, the cart rocking from their weight. Kenny shut the door and put his fingers on the ride. The music kicked in, and the carts went around.

Chaz and Julia panted, catching their breath.

"Oh, Jesus. I never want to move again," Chaz said.

The toddler quieted as Julia rocked him in her seat. The cart made its way to the pinnacle, and Chaz stared out at the park. The Spider-Walkers stayed at the midway line, screeching and slashing at nothing. Bloodied bodies dotted the walkway by the barns.

They all stayed silent for a little while. Kenny stared at them with a smile on his face.

Chaz broke the quiet. "I have a question."

Kenny said, "Yes?"

"If the spirits have realms they can't leave, why was I able to go wherever I wanted? And Julia and the toddler. All of us."

Kenny frowned. "It takes time before you're locked in."

"If we aren't locked in, how do you know we can't leave?"

Julia stepped in. "Trust me, we tried to get through that exit. We couldn't get out."

Kenny put his head down. "The entrance and exit are blocked. Someone put dark energy on them. But one time, I saw one of the guys who runs the games. He died, appeared, and walked right out the back where the fencing was broken. He never came back."

Chaz and Julia looked at each other.

"We need to go. Before we get locked in."

"But the guy who left had someone follow him," Kenny said, his eyes wide, trying to convince them to stay.

"What do you mean?"

"There used to be another spirit here. He followed the guy out. If you leave, you might let The Farmer out."

Chaz gave Julia a look. She nodded. "We'll risk it."

Kenny's eyelids sagged. "No. You can't leave me."

Julia touched his hand. "You just said the spirits can follow us out. You can leave, too."

Kenny shook his head. "No. The Farmer will kill me. I'm safe here."

Chaz cleared his throat. "Kid, you've been hiding on a Ferris wheel for decades. You can find your mom. You can live again."

Kenny shook his head. "I can't."

"Please bring us down," Julia asked.

Kenny shook his head more violently.

Chaz got in Kenny's face, wanting their eyes to connect. "You have the chance to save us."

He shook his head one more time.

Chaz sighed and opened the door. "Julia, I'm going to slide down this spoke, and then you hand me the kid and slide down yourself. We'll just keep doing that until we reach the bottom."

She nodded. "I'm not a fan of heights, but okay."

Tears formed in Kenny's eyes.

Chaz slid down. He gave a quick scan for The Giant, not seeing him anywhere. Julia hung out of the cart and handed Chaz the toddler. He nodded and slid as far along the crossbar as possible to give Julia room to slide down.

Once she reached his level, he handed the toddler back and slid down the next spoke. They repeated this until they reached the controller's station.

"Okay, when we hop down, we need to run as fast as we can to that section over there." Chaz pointed to where the porta toilets were. There was a break in the fence, and even from here, Chaz could see all the cigarette butts on the dirt outside it. He guessed the folks working the fair used it to sneak out for the occasional smoke.

Julia nodded. "Okay, let's do this. Where's your car? My boyfriend drove us in, and I don't have the keys."

Chaz pointed to the area where his car would be. "It's down there somewhere. It's a blue Plymouth Reliant."

She nodded again. "Okay, got it."

"One." Chaz wiped the sweat from his palms. "Two." He took a deep breath.

"NEEEEEEEEEWWWWWWWWW BLOOD."

Bang. Bang. Bang.

Kenny yelled from his cart. "NEEEEEEEWWWWWWWW BLOOD."

"That fucking kid," Chaz said.

Bang. The Giant's footsteps came from behind them.

"RUN!" Julia yelled.

They both charged for the fence.

The Giant's steps came closer, running right for them.

A knife flew into one of the porta toilets. Julia turned sideways and slid through the opening in the fence. As Chaz waited for her to get out of the way, The Giant came closer. Closer.

Just as the space in the fence opened up for him, the full weight of The Giant crashed into him. They both tumbled through the opening into the parking lot, The Giant landing hard on top of Chaz.

The gray disappeared and the world turned bright again. The colors seemed so much sharper now that Chaz had been deprived of them for hours. It was dark, though, night having crept in while he was away.

The lot was nearly empty. Only about fifty cars remained,

all far away from each other. Probably workers cleaning up after the place cleared out from the shooting. Hours must have passed. Police and ambulances were long gone.

As Chaz squirmed from under his attacker, The Giant grabbed Chaz's foot and pulled him closer. With his free foot, Chaz kicked him in the face. The man squealed as his sickle-shaped teeth cracked.

Julia ran over and helped Chaz up, holding the toddler in her other arm. They ran through the muddy parking lot, pockmarked with giant divots and uneven terrain.

They got about fifty feet before The Giant was back up, but that was all they needed. Chaz spotted his car and pointed at it for Julia to see. When they reached it, The Giant had closed the distance between them, but Chaz had time to hop in and unlock the passenger door. Julia slid in the passenger seat and buckled herself in, squeezing the toddler close to her chest.

"GO!"

Chaz turned the key and the engine roared. A knife flew at the windshield. The point hit hard, creating a dot that spider-webbed a few inches in each direction.

Chaz hit the gas, but the wheels spun in the mud. Of course. The Giant jumped on top of the hood, digging his knife into it.

Chaz pressed harder on the gas. The wheels spun out and the engine growled louder.

The Giant's meaty fist slammed onto the windshield and the glass made another spiderweb.

"Come on. Come on," Chaz said.

Julia's legs shook. "Get us out."

The gas pedal hit the floor, and with a jerk, the wheels broke free from the mud and The Giant rolled off the car. The car bumped and bounced along the pockmarks. The toddler cried again, not enjoying the ride.

With the lot so empty, Chaz didn't mind hitting the gas

hard. There was nothing to crash into. The front tires jerked a few times, and he had to spin the wheel forcefully to keep them on track, but otherwise, they sped away onto the hill with ease. The Giant hadn't given up his chase, but distance grew between them.

When they hit the hill, which was much easier going down, The Giant stopped at the top.

Chaz watched him get smaller in the rearview.

He drove out of the fairgrounds and onto the main road, his heart pounding hard in his chest, but as the lights of the Ferris wheel disappeared behind the oaks, he eased his fingers on the steering wheel.

"Where do I take you?" Chaz asked.

She gave him her address. "I'll have to look up who this guy's parents are. I have no idea how I'll explain he's alive when they saw his dead body."

"I think you don't explain it. Let them come up with their stories. Miracles. God. Whatever they need. It won't matter. All they'll care about is having him back."

She nodded.

Chaz dropped her off at her house, and rolled away into the night, heading home. He couldn't believe it. He was going home.

He called out of work for the week and waited three days before he struck up the nerve to call Jess. He lay on his bed staring at the ceiling as the phone rang. She picked up but didn't say anything for a few seconds. Neither knew how to break that barrier. Finally, she said, "Chaz?"

"Yeah. You owe me a sleepover."

She laughed. "Holy fuck. You made it out." She sniffled. "I started to lose hope."

"I'm not gonna lie, I'm a little pissed at you right now. I

heard you yelling at your cousin, and I know you didn't ask for any of that to happen, but in my mind, I can't help but blame you a little."

She breathed heavily into the phone. "Yeah. I get it. I never would have asked you to do that. All I can ask is that you know that."

"If we ever go on another date, and things work out, I don't ever want to meet your family, okay? Because I will punch your cousin in his face."

She laughed. "Well, he deserves that, but he also saved you."

Chaz sat up. "What do you mean?"

"He gave you that necklace. It's the only way out of the fair when you die there. You and anything close to it can escape."

Chaz looked over at the necklace resting on his nightstand. Kenny had it wrong. There was no escape from the fair. Only the necklace could do it. That's why the rest of them couldn't leave from the exit. That's why The Giant was able to follow Chaz out but couldn't get down the hill once the car got a good lead on him. That fucker had lost his closeness to the necklace. Julia and the toddler made it out because they stayed with Chaz the whole time.

"Let me guess, your cousin knew about the necklace from experience?"

"Yeah, and the idiot brought some bad shit back with him. But he's all into that dark arts stuff and was able to get rid of the spirit that followed him."

Chaz rested his head back on his pillow. "Damn."

ONE YEAR LATER

Jess opted not to return to the fairgrounds, for obvious reasons, so Chaz stood in line at the Ferris wheel by himself.

When he reached the controller's station, he said, "Can you let the next person on? I want to get on cart six."

The guy shrugged and let the couple behind Chaz get on ahead of him. When cart six came down, Chaz got in.

It moved one place forward while the next set of people got on.

"Can you see me?" Chaz said. "Make the cart shake if you can see and hear me."

Nothing.

He tried again, and again. Nothing. When they reached the pinnacle, he looked out at the fair. He hated crowds now more than ever, but he looked at the people playing games, laughing with their children, cuddling with their significant others, and he smiled. Then the smile turned into laughter.

As he laughed, the cart shook. Then he remembered Kenny saying the spirits can sense happiness. He knew the boy could see him now.

"I found your parents. Looked up who you were as soon as I got home, and then found your mom and dad. They're still alive. And I know they miss you more than anything in the world. I don't know how the hell we're going to explain to them that their son, who died decades ago, is still the same age, but we'll figure something out. I gotta try though. I have to."

He pulled out a knife and jabbed it into his throat.

A few minutes later, he opened his eyes to a world turned gray. Across from him in the cart, Kenny smiled.

"You ready to get out of here?"

Kenny nodded, smiled, and laughed. "You came back."

"Not gonna lie, I'm not happy with you after you yelled 'new blood' on us, but yeah, I came back."

Kenny leaped across the cart and hugged him. "Take me home."

"You got it." He hugged the boy. "You got it."

I inherited my mother's anxiety, and while I've lived with that my whole life, as I've gotten older, my fear of public places (especially crowded ones) has intensified. Her agoraphobia kept her from doing a lot of things she loved, and I work hard to not let that happen to me. But when I'm in a space with a lot of people, my mind focuses on who could be a potential threat. I check the nearest exits, the pathways to escape through if something goes down. I hate being that paranoid, but it's a reality for me, and the more news stories I see about mass public shootings, the more I feel that way.

I didn't want to write a story that focused on that, though. Yes, I wanted to show the fear in it, but I wanted the story to be about something else. I love carnival horror, and there's a lot of it, but I haven't seen much that uses the fair setting. Not clowns, but the small stuff. The egg tosses and the line dancing and the antique barns and the spotlights on local farmers.

And I wanted to make it horrifying. I like being known as an author where the reader never feels safe, that their favorite character might not make it out. But in this one, I knew from the beginning I wanted the children to find salvation, to get a second chance, because too often when I flick on the news, that's not the case. And a piece of me dies every time I see it.

Thanks for checking out my stories. I hope you enjoyed them. I hope you cried. I hope you got a little scared. I hope you wake up tomorrow feeling a little closer to yourself, a little more at peace with the darkness in the world around you.

Welcome to DreadPop.

JOIN THE CULT:

HTTPS://WWW.PATREON.COM/GAGEGREENWOOD

STAND ALONE NOVELS:

Bunker Dogs

On a Clear Day, You Can See Block Island

In the Eyes, In the Shadows (October 2024)

We Are All Dead, Anyway (COMING 2025)

THE WINTER SAGA

Winter's Myths

Winter's Legacy

Winter's End (COMING SOON)

SHORT STORIES

Grackles on the Feeder

Through Flickering Lights, a Silhouette

ABOUT THE AUTHOR

Gage Greenwood is the best-selling author of the Winter's Myths Saga, and Bunker Dogs. He's a proud member of the Horror Writers Association and Science Fiction and Fantasy Writers association.

He's been an actor, comedian, podcaster, and even the Vice President of an escape room company. Since childhood, he's been a big fan of comic books, horror movies, and depressing music that fills him with existential dread.

He lives in New England with his girlfriend and son, and he spends his time writing, hiking, and decorating for various holidays.

Find out more, or contact me: www.gagegreenwood.com

facebook.com/gagegreenwoodauthor

instagram.com/gagegreenwood

patreon.com/gagegreenwood

threads.net/@gagegreenwood

tiktok.com/@gagegreenwoodauthor